"Destiny is a small town with real people living normal lives.

They worry about keeping their jobs, paying their bills and finding a way to put their kids through college. But you know all that, Bobby, because you once lived in this town. Back when you made a promise not to set foot in it again until you could return a big success with all the money in the world."

An icy wave coursed through him, despite the warmth of the sun hitting his back. Yes, he'd said all that—and more—the day she'd chosen a shot at the glamorous life of high fashion modeling over being his teenage bride.

"What can I say?" His reply came out clipped, sharp as a shard of glass. "Mission accomplished."

Dear Reader,

In this age of technology that allows people to connect across the miles and across the years, there probably isn't much mystery left to that old question, "I wonder whatever happened to…" When it comes to first loves, the answer is usually a click away, but for some avoidance is the only answer.

When Leeann and Bobby's future plans took their teenage love in a direction neither of them planned, the last thing they expected was to one day end up right back where it all began. But sometimes love, and life, surprises a person in a way they never imagined.

So is an unexpected reunion an opportunity to set the record straight, right old wrongs, offer explanations with the insight only available after time has passed? Or is it another chance to find that part of yourself that's been missing all along?

Leeann and Bobby are about to find out.

Happy Reading!

Christyne Butler

Welcome Home,
Bobby Winslow

CHRISTYNE BUTLER

First published in Great Britain 2012
by Mills & Boon, an imprint of Harlequin (UK) Limited.
Large Print edition 2012
Harlequin (UK) Limited,
Eton House, 18-24 Paradise Road,
Richmond, Surrey TW9 1SR

© Christyne Butilier 2011

ISBN: 978 0 263 23021 5

Printed and bound in Great Britain
by CPI Antony Rowe, Chippenham, Wiltshire

CHRISTYNE BUTLER

fell in love with romance novels while serving in the United States Navy and started writing her own stories six years ago. She considers selling to Special Edition a dream come true and enjoys writing contemporary romances full of life, love, a hint of laughter and perhaps a dash of danger, too. And there has to be a happily-ever-after or she's just not satisfied.

She lives with her family in central Massachusetts and loves to hear from her readers at chris@christynebutler.com. Or visit her website at www.christynebutler.com

For Tammy Gerard Hastings

Thirty-one years of friendship
that's seen everything from
first loves to new beginnings.

Here's to always believing
it's never too late to live happily ever after.

and

Extra special thanks to Charles
for being such an amazing editor.

Chapter One

Bobby Winslow was back in town.

According to the front page of the local paper there had yet to be an official sighting of the man who'd been voted "Best Hands (When it comes to working on cars)" in high school. But that didn't matter. The reporter was certain the town's bad boy, who'd spent the past six years rising to the number one spot in America's Cup Pro Racing stock car circuit, was on his way home.

Deputy Leeann Harris gave an indelicate snort

and tossed the newspaper into the backseat of her cruiser.

She had to.

Otherwise she'd be tempted to take her eyes off the curvy mountain road to look again at the photos beneath the bold headline, including one taken just a few days ago when Bobby had been wheeled out of an injury rehabilitation center; it was the first time he'd been seen in five months. He'd struggled to his feet and spoken briefly, thanking those who took care of him after his accident and stating he was looking forward to continuing his recovery at home.

Home.

Everyone around town assumed that meant Destiny, Wyoming.

Never mind that Bobby had left at the age of eighteen with a vow to never step foot back inside the county limits. A vow made during a fervent outburst filled with the hurt and anger of a broken teenage heart.

A vow directed straight at her.

Of course, she'd made her own vow that spring day fourteen years ago.

This time it took the physical shaking of her head to force Leeann's mind back to the road ahead, both figuratively and literally.

She refused to get mired down in the past. Not today.

Using a technique she'd learned long ago to center herself in the here and now, Leeann mentally cataloged her surroundings starting with the beautiful late September day outside her windshield.

The sky was a dazzling shade of blue, sharp and piercing, perfect for squinting eyes and almost impossible to look away from. Birch, ash and maple trees stood tall and majestic on either side of the road. Their green leaves were giving way to the blazing yellows, oranges and fiery reds of autumn, while the smattering of pines and blue spruces stubbornly refused to let go of their glorious emerald needles.

The winding road wore a fresh coat of blacktop, like it'd pulled on a warm woolen jacket in preparation for another Wyoming winter of snow and ice. But when she rolled down the window and pulled in a deep breath, the air still held the lingering warmth of summer.

"What a beautiful day to be unemployed," she said to herself. Technically she wasn't out of work until her shift ended in—she glanced at her watch—two more hours. After that, her three years with the Destiny, Wyoming, sheriff department would come to an end.

Budget cuts. Last hired, first fired. Well, that wasn't entirely true. Deputy Ben Dwyer had started a full month after her, but with a wife and two kids, Ben needed to keep his job. When word leaked out about the need to cut the department's staff by one, Leeann had gone straight into her boss's office.

It was time.

Moving on was something she'd been thinking about for a while now. After witnessing her two best friends finding true love with the men of their dreams and settling down in the past year, she was willing to admit, at least to herself, she was feeling a bit restless. Not for love, home or marriage like Maggie and Racy had found, but she did want something.

Something more.

Like those many "forks in the road" her Aunt Ursula often spoke about, Leeann was ready to take the path less traveled with no idea where she was headed or what lay ahead.

The story of her life.

Pulling off the road to her favorite waiting spot that gave her a clear view down the mountain road, she slowed to a stop.

She hoped the remaining hours of her shift would be quiet, but the high school had let out almost a half hour ago. This stretch of windy road was a teenager paradise for cruising, especially on a beautiful day like today, just like it'd been years ago when she'd rode shotgun, a smile on her face and a white-knuckle grip on the seat while—

A loud whoosh filled her ears. An oversize vehicle raced by so fast the draft caused the chassis beneath her to rock back and forth.

What the—

Was that a Winnebago?

Leeann flipped on her lights and siren and tore out after the jumbo motor home as it disappeared around the first turn. She lost sight of it, but there was nowhere for a vehicle that size to turn off for a least a mile. She pressed on the accelerator and roared over the next small hill, spotting the RV ahead as it pulled to the side of the road.

With no room to move in behind, she was forced to park in front, angling her cruiser nose in. Keeping an eye on her rearview mirror, she finished her call to dispatch that included the North Carolina license plate number and stepped out of the car.

Pushing her short hair back from her face, Leeann settled the Destiny Sheriff Department ball cap on her head.

Tourists. Probably a senior citizen with a lead foot.

She paused at the rear of her car, one hand inches from her weapon, and assessed the situation. Nice and quiet. So far, so good, except that thanks to the angle of the sun she couldn't make out the people inside the camper other than the fact there were two of them. At least.

She moved a few steps closer, motioning with one hand.

The driver understood and slid his window open. "Is there a problem, Officer?"

Okay, that was no grandpa.

The man leaning out the window had cropped salt-and-pepper hair and dark sunglasses obscuring his eyes. His arm was bigger than her thigh. The sleeve of his black T-shirt hugged the well-developed biceps, revealing a tattoo she couldn't quite make out.

"Please step out of the vehicle." There was no way she was dealing with this guy from where he sat three feet above her. "And bring your license and registration with you."

"I'm going to have to use the rear door." He patted the smooth surface beneath his hand. "We're having trouble with this one."

"Fine."

He offered a quick grin and ducked back inside.

Leeann watched as he talked to his passenger, gesturing with his hands before he moved out of his seat and disappeared from view. She walked back along the side of her cruiser, keeping it between her and the camper.

Eyeing the motor home, she noticed it looked brand-new and custom-made with its fancy paint job and tinted windows, but she was still surprised at how it'd zoomed by her.

The shade from tall trees to her left made it easier to see, and she paused on the other side of her car, her gaze on the person still sitting in the front of the camper.

A man, also wearing sunglasses, his with mirrored lenses, and a weathered ball cap on his head turned backward. He'd glanced her way through the window.

Seconds later, he did the classic double take.

Leeann held her ground and his gaze. Thanks to his sunglasses she couldn't be sure, but instinct and years of experience told her he was checking her out from the top of her ball cap to the tips of her steel-toed boots.

His scrutiny caused a heated flush to steal over her skin. It'd been many years since she'd had a physical reaction to a man's gaze. A tinge of annoyance mixed with the surprise coursing through her.

Why now? Why him?

Did she somehow know this guy?

No, that was crazy.

The stranger finally turned away and she blamed her body's response on the warmth of the Indian summer afternoon.

Still, it'd been a long time since she'd gotten that kind of response from someone. When she'd first started working as a deputy sheriff, it had happened often when she pulled someone over, be it a local or an out-of-town tourist who recognized her. But other than one of those celebrity magazines doing a "where are they now" profile on her a couple of years ago, Leeann was far removed from the bright lights and big city of her former life.

Did he know who she was? Or, more precisely, who she used to be?

Maybe he just didn't like the law. Except the tiny hitch that pulled at one corner of his mouth had her thinking he'd been about to smile. To flirt his way out of a ticket?

Just then the rear door of the camper opened and out stepped a giant of a man.

He was easily over six feet tall, the rest of him as powerfully put together as that one arm he'd displayed out the window. The black T-shirt stretched tautly over his wide chest, matching black jeans fit him like a second skin and the scuffed work boots gave him a couple of extra unnecessary inches in height.

He walked toward her, his gaze locked with hers. Other than her usual watchfulness that was part of the job, she felt none of the physical effects from a moment ago during that silent exchange with his passenger.

With no time to figure out why, Leeann pushed the thought aside when the driver stopped a few feet from her. He offered another grin that appeared too good-hearted to be artificial and held out his hand.

She took the paperwork, looked at his driver's license first then glanced back at him. "Dean Zippenella?"

"Yes, ma'am."

The picture on the New Jersey license matched the man in front of her, but his full name? "Dean Martin Zippenella?"

His grin widened as he shrugged. "I come from a large Italian family and my Nonni was a big fan. Most people call me Zip or Zippy."

"You should meet his brothers Frank and Joey."

Leeann glanced up as the guy still in the camper spoke. That voice. Barely above a whisper, and still the measured tone easily carried across the distance to where she stood. She hated to say it sounded familiar, because it didn't, but still a nugget of awareness tugged inside her.

She then noticed the dog in his lap, its two front paws on the window frame. Bland canine features spoke of a mongrel heritage and its coat was a mix of browns and tans, except for the solid patch of black over one eye.

"As in Frank Sinatra and Joey Bishop?" she said, looking between the two men.

Both nodded.

"Which one are you?" she asked the guy in the camper.

"Huh?" The hand scratching at the dog's ears stilled.

"Are you two related?" she pushed.

"No."

"Yes."

Their overlapping answers had her moving her gaze back and forth in suspicion. "Is my question too confusing?"

The driver crossed his arms over the impressive width of his chest. "We're not blood, but we're close as family can be."

Leeann tilted her head to one side, hoping Jersey got her unspoken message. If he was going for intimidation, it wasn't going to help his cause. He dropped his arms.

"What does it matter?" The man in the camper spoke again, his voice still low but now with a harder edge to it. "And why pull us over? We weren't over the posted speed limit."

Much.

The unspoken end of his sentence hung in the air.

"Look, I'm getting a bit tired of going back and forth between you two. Why don't you join your friend out here? And leave Fido inside."

He stared at her again until Leeann broke from his gaze to look back to his friend, ignoring the persistent internal whisper that she somehow knew this stranger.

"Is that really necessary, Officer Harris?" he asked.

The use of her name caused Leeann's head to snap back toward him.

The tone of his voice sounded different now. Softer. Almost recognizable.

Why had he called her by name? Could he make out the letters on the small tag attached to the front of her uniform?

She swallowed hard against the lump in her throat. "Yes, it's necessary."

He looked away and this time his gaze held with his traveling companion's. Leeann glanced over in time to see the Rat Pack namesake give his head a slight shake.

"On my way," the Smart Mouth finally replied, pulling the dog back inside and swinging his oversize bucket seat away from the window.

The driver sighed.

Leeann focused her attention on him again,

wondering why he didn't want his friend out here.

"Her name is Daisy," the muscleman said, his grin back. "The dog? She's mine and her name is Daisy. After Daisy Duke. The hottie from *The Dukes of Hazzard?*"

Leeann fought back a grin and the urge to roll her eyes. "Yes, I know the show. Is anyone else inside the camper?"

"Nope, just the three of us."

She nodded, feeling at ease with the big guy. Still, she continued her silent count, which had started when she'd asked his buddy to come outside.

She soon reached one-eighty, approximately three minutes. The driver kept looking at the camper's side door and shifting his weight, as if he wanted to go and see what was taking his friend so long. Another few minutes passed before the door finally opened.

The man gingerly stepped down, starting toward them in slow, measured steps. She immediately wondered if he was under the influence as he fought to keep his balance.

Unlike his buddy, this guy's clothes seemed to hang off him, despite his tall frame and the width of his shoulders. His white cotton shirt was wrinkled and hung loosely over baggy jeans. His sneakered feet shuffled through the dirt as if he had to work hard to put one foot in front of the other.

He'd turned his ball cap around, the brim now low on his forehead, allowing her to only see the flat press of his lips. In anger? No, this guy was in pain.

When he finally reached them, a fine sheen of sweat glistened on his face and throat.

"Are you okay?" she asked.

His head jerked in a quick nod as he ran a hand across his chest, pulling the soft material taut.

"Can I see your driver's license, please?"

This time he offered a halfhearted laugh and her heart flinched. Then he removed his ball cap and slid off his glasses, his mouth relaxing in a halfhearted smile.

"It hasn't been that long, has it, Leeann?"

The air vanished from her lungs as her heart froze.

Bobby Winslow.

Alive and well and standing right in front of her.

Gone was the belligerent stranger and in his place stood the man she had once promised to marry.

The newspaper hadn't lied.

Bobby really was back in town and looking pretty much the same as he had at eighteen. His hair was still dark and wavy with a cowlick that fell across his forehead. Straight white teeth flashed when he spoke, and the twin dimples she remembered threatened to appear during his lethargic attempt at a smile.

For a quick moment, a sparkle lit his familiar blue eyes, equal parts pirate rogue and boyish charm, before he blinked and the emotion disappeared.

The black-and-white pictures in the newspaper had masked the true effect of his charisma, but Leeann knew firsthand how overwhelming Bobby's eyes, though dim and shuttered now, could be.

At fifteen, she'd been powerless against them.

At thirty-two, they still turned her knees to mush. Knees she locked to keep upright.

He was waiting for a response.

Leeann said the first thing that popped into her head. "You look a bit worse for wear."

"Well, that gets right to the heart of things." Bobby shoved his hands into his back pockets, the cap and glasses dangling from his fingers. "Same ol' Lee."

He'd been the only one who'd gotten away with shortening her name. Something she'd always hated until the time he'd said it, right before he kissed her in the oversize backseat of his '71 Duster at the drive-in.

"I didn't—I didn't mean it like that." Leeann's words rushed past her lips. "You look good… well, considering you've only been—"

"Sprung from rehab less than a week." Bobby cut her off with a wave of a hand, the action causing him to sway. He cocked one hip and steadied himself. "Yeah, I'm not doing too badly for a guy who nearly died five months ago."

This time the tugging at her heart caused it to flip over completely. "Wh-what are you doing here?"

"I live here."

No, he didn't, not anymore.

Never mind the fact that Bobby's mother still lived in town, just a few houses away from Leeann in a cute cottage complete with a beautiful garden and a white picket fence that Bobby had bought for her with his winnings from his first major race.

Valzora Winslow had shared that little tidbit with pride when she'd surprised Leeann with a plate of freshly baked cookies as a housewarming gift the day Leeann had moved out of her aunt's place and into a home of her own.

They'd struck up a sociable wave-as-you-go-by friendship, often stopping to chat over the fence about simple things like the weather or the activities going on in Destiny.

But never about Leeann and Bobby's past.

So where was Val now that Bobby was back in town?

Instead of asking, Leeann stated the obvious, "You haven't lived here for over a decade."

"Neither have you," he countered.

How did he know that? They certainly hadn't kept in touch over the years and she doubted he was a fan of high fashion, even when that had been her life. "I've been back in town for three years, living on Laurel Lane for the last two."

Surprise flickered in his eyes as he put the name of her street together with his mother's. If that surprised him, he'd be shocked to know that Leeann had driven his mom to the airport the night of his accident.

"Destiny is my home," he replied with a vague thrust of his chin, the surprise now replaced with a hint of smugness. "And I'm here to check out my new digs just up the road."

The new digs being the monstrous log mansion constructed over the summer. The rumor that the multimillion-dollar house was owned by the town's favorite son had been confirmed in another newspaper article back in July.

Leeann hadn't gone anywhere near the construction, dubbed "Castle Winslow" by the locals, especially after she'd learned who owned the company that had purchased *her* land months earlier.

"Well, at least your appearance explains the speed of your oversize home on wheels." She waved at the camper, latching on to a familiar topic. "You never could resist tinkering with an engine. How much have you messed with the inner workings of that thing?"

"It's a 362-horsepower 6.8 liter Super Duty V10 SEFI Triton engine and I haven't done anything to it," he said, with another hint of his familiar grin. "Yet."

"You sure? You two were hauling butt." Leeann handed the paperwork and license back to his friend, but kept her gaze on Bobby as a thought came to her. "Or maybe it wasn't your friend here who was behind the wheel. Maybe it was you."

The grin disappeared. "Believe me, I wasn't driving."

Less than seventy-two hours away from a rehabilitation center, probably not. Still, he was standing under his own power.

"I don't recall too many times when you willingly sat shotgun," she said.

"No, if memory serves, that spot usually belonged to my girlfriend."

A low hum of fury at his mocking tone passed through her. She fought to keep her next words light. "So you've learned to share now?"

Bobby cocked his head to one side and his grin

returned. "Only out of necessity. You know how I hate to give up a position of power."

Power behind the wheel, power over her.

From the start of their teenage relationship, Leeann had never been able to resist the magnetic pull Bobby had over her. She'd been drawn to his wild, untamed and cocky personality from the moment they met. Maybe because he was so different from the starched and conventional home life she had with her parents.

Being with Bobby gave her a freedom she'd never known before, even after he'd surprised her with an engagement ring in February of their senior year and convinced her that getting married right after graduation was the best way to be together.

"Yes, I remember. It took having a diamond ring flung at your head before you finally took 'no' for an answer."

His smile vanished as soon as the words left her mouth.

Leeann couldn't believe she'd said that aloud and in front of an innocent bystander.

"I'm sorry, that wasn't fair—"

"Don't worry about it." He cut her off with a wave of his hand. "I think we've had enough apologies between us to last a lifetime."

His sharp tone brought back the memory instantly.

Not far from this very spot, between tears and apologies, she'd tried to explain why she'd decided to leave town.

Alone.

Why she'd accepted a modeling contract in New York City, the prize for winning a contest she hadn't known her mother had entered Leeann into.

Why she'd changed her mind about marrying him before he was set to leave for the U.S. Army the week after their high school graduation. A ceremony that had only been days away.

Boy, he must've waited years to throw her words back in her face.

Leeann swallowed hard against an old ache she'd thought was long buried. Instead, she pasted on a counterfeit smile, honed to perfection from years in front of the camera. "Okay, well, let's consider this a warning for both of you."

She looked at Bobby's friend, who'd remained quiet during this whole exchange. "Please obey the speed limits during your stay, Mr. Zippenella."

"Yes, ma'am," the man replied, shoving his license into his wallet before pocketing it. "But you can still call me Dean. Or Zippy. Hell, I'll answer if you yell out a simple 'hey you.'"

Leeann's smile slipped from fake to genuine with ease. Boy, this guy had his namesake's charm in spades. "I'll keep that in mind, Dean."

"So, are we free to go, Officer?"

Stepping back toward her cruiser, Leeann glanced at Bobby again, noticing a slight trembling in his ramrod-straight posture and a growing gleam of sweat dotting his skin.

An urge to ask again if he was okay filled her, but she quickly squashed it as she headed for the driver's-side door. "Yes, gentleman, you are. Enjoy the rest of this beautiful fall day. And Bobby...welcome home."

Chapter Two

Bobby dropped his arms, the movement causing him to sway again. Bracing his hands on his hips, he kept his eyes trained on Leeann's cruiser until it disappeared over the hill.

A familiar shaking of his legs warned him that the searing pain he'd learned to live with over the past few months was fast approaching. He managed six steps toward the camper before his strength gave out and he crumpled into a heap near the front tire.

Zippy raced to his side, crouching next to him. "Dammit, Ace!"

Bobby's gaze remained on the empty black-top, his brain still trying to process the fact that the girl who'd walked away from their foolish teenage dreams in order to become a successful model was back in Destiny.

And working as a deputy sheriff.

If not for that low sexy voice of hers, smoky and smooth like the whiskey he'd come to favor over the years, he never would've believed his first love was the same person who'd stood in front of him in a khaki uniform, her once-famous waist-length hair now so short it barely brushed her shoulders.

A cop?

Really?

"Hey, bro?" Zip gave him a gentle nudge. "You okay?"

Bobby shook his head, mentally pushing away the long-ago sealed memories before they had a chance to form. Instead he concentrated on the blinding rush that felt like a thousand pricks of hot needles radiating from his hips to his knees.

"Yeah, I'm good." He pushed the words past gritted teeth. "I'm great."

"No, what you are is stupid. She obviously knew about your accident. You could've had your little reunion through the window." Zip wrapped one beefy arm around his back, providing a strong and steady presence.

Just like he'd done from the moment Bobby first opened his eyes in the hospital after the accident. Like he'd done the day they'd met in a desert hellhole ten years ago.

"Why didn't you stay inside the camper?" Zip asked.

No way.

It took a full-on stare at Leeann for Bobby to match the girl to her voice. No, make that woman. Long gone was the girly-girl he'd known in high school who'd entered beauty pageant after beauty pageant and barely had the strength to carry her own books.

When he'd finally realized who'd pulled them over, he'd been determined to meet Leeann Harris again for the first time face-to-face and standing unaided on his own two feet.

"So that was her," Zip said.

Bobby looked at his friend and blinked. "Huh?"

"You know, beauty queen, first love, heartbreaker, high-rent cover model for *Cosmo, Vogue, Brides*—"

"Damn you and your steel-trap memory." Bobby bent his knees and braced his feet in the dirt. "Help me get off my ass."

Zip managed to shrug while shouldering Bobby's weight and helping him back to a standing position. "With all the boo-hooing you did that night, how could I forget?"

Thankful the pain was fading already, Bobby leaned against the camper. He wasn't ready to try walking yet. "We drank a lot that night."

"We were celebrating finally being back on American soil." Zip dropped his hold and stepped back, but stayed close. "Drinking for those who never came home."

Bobby remembered.

Their first night back after a front-row seat in the Middle East during that "quiet" time between the first Gulf War and the second, courtesy of the U.S. Army. The only two guys in their unit who hadn't had anyone to go home to, he and Zip had ended up shutting down a hole-in-the-wall bar outside the gates of Fort Bragg. Then they'd stumbled to a nearby motel to continue drinking and talking until the sun rose.

"You know, Ace, if you were so dogged to come out of the camper on your own power, you could've at least grabbed a—"

"Let it go, Zip. It's done and over."

"Famous last words."

Bobby glared at his friend. "She's gone."

"Yeah. For now. But if I remember correctly from all of your stories, Destiny is a pretty small town."

Meaning he and Leeann would run into each other again.

Maybe.

Probably.

But next time, Bobby would be prepared.

He dropped his head back against the cool metal of the custom motor home he'd had built a year ago. It was supposed to have been his ride during this past season's race calendar. Now it was a high-priced ambulance bringing him home.

"Come on, Zip, let's get moving. I want to finally see in person what my hard-earned greenbacks have been paying for all summer."

"Meaning all those photos, live video feeds and the miniature model you had sent to the rehab hospital weren't enough?"

Since he was a kid, first attending and then working summers at a local wilderness camp, Bobby had always wanted to live in a log cabin. He just never thought it would be here in Destiny. Then fate had allowed him to keep a long-held promise.

He'd approved the plans for his upscale and oversize version back in February, but by the time of his accident in May, only half of the outer shell was complete. He'd watched the rest of the construction from his hospital bed.

"No, they weren't nearly enough." He looked at his friend's grinning face while shoving his hat back on his head and pocketing his sunglasses. "And you knew that before you asked."

"Yeah, I did." Zip moved to his side. "You okay to walk?"

Gripping his friend's oversize forearm, Bobby slowly put one foot in front of the other. The stinging had lessened, but the needling sensation had moved down to his feet. Sort of like when a person sat too long and tingled when he first moved.

Only about twenty times worse.

"With a bit of help," he grunted around clenched teeth.

"That's what I'm here for, bud. A promise is a promise."

"Knock it off with that promise stuff, would ya?" Bobby shot back. "I've told you how I feel about that."

"And when was the last time I ever listened to you?"

"Three years ago. At your family's place in Jersey." Bobby gripped the handrail and hefted himself inside, conscious of his buddy behind him, ready to catch him if he fell. Which he didn't do much anymore despite what had just happened.

"I agreed with your sisters, and Frank and Joey." He kept talking. It seemed to speed up his recovery from these episodes. Or at least distracted him. "That girl you'd brought home was all wrong for you."

"And perfect for Frankie," Zip said with a wry twist of his lips.

Bobby purposely shuffled past the dining set and leather sectional sofa where Daisy lounged, her snout on her paws as she watched them. That dog always knew when to stay out of the way. A skill most likely learned in the war zone where Zip had found her.

Thankful when he reached the cushioned passenger seat, Bobby eased into it with a silent sigh. "Yeah, especially when we caught her and Frankie going at it in the backyard gazebo."

"That wasn't my brother's fault." Zip moved back behind the steering wheel. "He was young and stupid."

"He was twenty-three." Bobby pulled on his seat belt. "And yet you still made a show of knocking him through the screen door."

"Hey, my pride was at stake."

"And you made sure the girl got home okay. Even Daisy didn't want anything to do with her."

Zip shrugged, buckled his seat belt as well and started the engine. "Daisy doesn't like any females. Never has, unlike me. What can I say? I was in love *and* stupid. Runs in the family, right?"

Yeah, Bobby and Zip might not be blood, but they were family just the same.

"Drive, bro." Bobby kept his gaze on the road and ran his hands along the tops of his thighs, kneading at the tight muscles. "I'm ready to go home."

By nine the next morning, Bobby felt much better.

If better meant enduring a morning physical therapy session that twisted him inside out and upside down. They'd finished the workout by christening the new indoor pool with a race Zip had won, barely, and twenty minutes in the steam room.

Now fresh from the shower and dressed, Bobby palmed a cup of hot coffee as he sat in his office. He leaned back in his chair and stared out the window at the acres of trees surrounding his new home.

That was a lot of green.

And gold and orange and red and burgundy. Fall in Wyoming. His favorite season.

He'd grown up the child of a single mother, his father gone before Bobby had started kindergarten. They'd lived in a third-floor, two-bedroom apartment located in the center of town next to Mason's Garage.

Despite Destiny being a small place, it had plenty of parks, fairgrounds and wide-open spaces, but Bobby had always longed for a tree-filled yard of his own.

He finally had it—and it was a yard that once had belonged to Leeann.

A yard where her family's Georgian-style mansion, the home she'd grown up in, stood, until an electric storm set fire to the empty house.

He'd only been out to the Harris home a few times when he was young, but he'd never been allowed inside. Her parents had forbidden Leeann to invite him in.

Not that he'd stayed away entirely.

A nearby pond, which hadn't been visible

from the Harris house and still couldn't be seen through the thick forest of trees, was a favorite meeting spot for him and Lee.

Deep in the woods, with only a well-worn path far from the house marking the way, was a place they'd met when they wanted to be together.

To talk, to laugh, to fall in love. It was the place he'd asked Leeann to marry him on a snowy Valentine's Day with a cheap diamond chip of a ring.

A place that still belonged to his former fiancée.

When he'd heard from his mother that the Harris land was up for sale—one of the rare times she'd mentioned Leeann—he'd put his lawyers on the task of purchasing the property. Originally made up of thirty-five prime Wyoming acres he'd vowed as a teenager to one day own, it was only twenty-seven acres when the purchase went through.

Prophetic, as his race car was also number twenty-seven.

Leeann had held on to the remaining land, eight acres that included the pond. When he'd seen the final offer, he'd had to admit it gave him a warm feeling to know she'd wanted to keep that place for herself.

"There you are." Zip interrupted his thoughts as he walked into the office. "Jeez, we walked around this castle of yours three times last night and I'm still lost. I think you need to print some maps. I can't even find my dog."

"Daisy was sunning herself in the family room the last time I saw her. And you know this place like the back of your hand." Bobby swung around to face his friend. "You should, you studied the floor plans as much as I did this summer."

"As long as I can figure out how to find the kitchen, I'm golden." His buddy took a large bite from the apple in his hand. "So what's on the agenda today? Maybe bring a little life to this place?"

"What are you talking about?" Bobby put down his mug. "The house is perfect."

"Yeah, it's got more flat-screen televisions than a sports bar and the 'I love me' wall downstairs is cute, but it still looks like something out of a magazine."

"Displaying all those awards and honors wasn't my idea. Blame the decorators."

"Yeah, they did such a great job this place looks more like a museum than a—wait, what the heck is that?"

A red light recessed into the top of Bobby's desk flashed. He pressed his thumb over the glass and it went out.

Reaching for the handmade cane his mother had given him in the hospital when he'd first started walking again, Bobby heaved himself up. "Come on, I think you're going to like this."

At the far wall, he ran one hand along the edge of the commissioned oil painting of his race car until he found a hidden button.

A door-size portion of log wall slid silently to

the left, disappearing into a hollow opening in the wall. Bobby entered the room on the other side, his buddy tight on his heels.

"Okay, that was a little James Bondish." Zip stopped next to him. "What is all this?"

A double row of monitors lined the far wall, eight in total, which flashed live images of Bobby's home and land. "This is my security center. I can see what's going on 24/7 from the driveway to the ends of my property."

"Other than that fancy wood-and-iron gate we passed through, I didn't see any fencing. Jeez, I never even noticed the cameras."

"That 'fancy' gate is actually high-strength aluminum made to look like wood. The fencing is electronic, and the cameras wireless and well hidden. This is a state-of-the-art system Devlin Murphy put together."

"Is he part of Murphy Mountain Log Homes that built this place?"

Bobby nodded. "Same company. Dev heads the home security side of things."

"I know you had some troubles with that nutty fangirl last year, but still, isn't this a bit much?"

"That wasn't just a fangirl. I went downstairs one morning and found her fixing breakfast... after she broke in."

"And your overnight companion wasn't too happy to find another female in the house, if I remember the news reports correctly." Zip smiled. "Or was the catfight just a nasty rumor?"

It wasn't. Despite his fame and sometimes overzealous fans, it was Bobby's first brush with someone who'd broken the law to get close to him. "Let's just say I'm a bit more cautious nowadays."

"Even up here in the backwoods?"

Bobby nodded as he moved in to read the monitor on the desk. "Especially with the phase two I have planned."

"As curious as I am about this 'phase two' of yours, why exactly did that red light go off on your desk?" Zip walked to the wall of monitors and peered closely at them. "All I see out there is trees."

Remembering the instructions Dev had emailed him, Bobby pressed a key to move the update backward until he saw the half-dozen screen captures. He leaned in close, then closer still, his eyes fixed on images taken of the driveway, outside the main gate but definitely on his land.

"I'm going to go out and get some fresh air." Bobby left the room, closing the door behind his friend who'd followed him.

"I worked you over pretty good this morning. You're not walking so well, even with that cane," Zip said. "You plan on sticking to the deck?"

"Actually I'm going for a quick drive." Leaving his study, Bobby headed for the main hall, the tap of his cane echoing off the stone floor.

"Ace, you can't—"

"It's a four by four utility, Zip." He stopped and turned to his buddy, recognizing the man's serious professional-therapist face. "Nothing more than a tricked-out golf cart. Standard issue, no modifications done."

"I'll come with you. Let me get Daisy. She'd love to ride."

"I think I can handle this—the cart by myself."

Zip folded his arms and stared at him, but Bobby just returned his steady gaze. No way was he bringing his friend along. Not this time. This was something he wanted—no, something he *needed* to face on his own.

"Take your cell and call if you need…anything."

Bobby nodded and headed for the mudroom that led to the attached four-bay garage. Soon he was mobile, pleased he was able to handle the electric utility vehicle. He'd convinced a nurse at the rehab center to let him get behind the wheel of a cart used by the facility, but the results hadn't been so good.

Steering the machine to the far end of the barn, he slowed to a stop, his focus on the opening between the two oak trees no one else would notice.

No one but him and Leeann.

Leeann prided herself on not making bad decisions. Not anymore. Goodness knows she'd made more than her share in her lifetime, but for the past six years she'd worked hard not to repeat them.

Then this morning she'd made a doozy.

Maybe because she'd overslept, something she never did. Or it could be because she left the house for her morning run without something in her stomach.

She refused to consider that last night's decision to crack open her old cedar chest filled with long-forgotten mementos and memories could have anything to do with her heading for the pond.

Her pond.

She ran into the clearing at the water's edge, which offered some relief considering the rocky terrain she'd just covered. Gasping, she slowed to a walk. Deep breaths pulled in the familiar piney and earth scents as the fresh mountain air invaded her lungs and cooled her heated skin.

Pulling off her ball cap, she shook her hair loose and then peeled off her nylon windbreaker, dropping it to a natural bench formed from a pair of felled trees.

The same bench she'd been coming to since she was a little girl. First alone when she needed a place of her own where she could think, dream or just get away from her mother and her beauty pageant obsession. Then one day she'd noticed a scruffy-looking boy on a secondhand bike staring at her from the other side of her pond. She'd been thirteen and within an hour she'd fallen in love with Bobby Winslow.

Leeann willed away the memory, knowing it was crazy to come here now that Bobby was living just down the road, the road that technically belonged to him, but was her only access to this section of woodland.

Her daily runs didn't always bring her here, but she'd fallen into her runner zone quickly. Her feet had a mind of their own, easily eating up the miles, drawing her to the peace and comfort she'd always found here.

Until now.

Until Bobby came back to town.

She stopped her pacing, slapped her cap back on and rubbed at the ache in the center of her chest. Lacing her fingers behind her head and planting her feet shoulders-width apart, she pressed her elbows outward and stretched, staring at the thick grove of multicolored trees surrounding the still blue waters.

Despite all the craziness that was her life, this calm oasis was still hers and she'd be damned if anyone was going to keep her away.

Dropping her arms, she stepped her feet together and bent at the waist. Hands curled around her ankles, she touched her forehead to her knees.

Deep breath in, deep breath out.

Eyes closed, she thought again about the events of yesterday afternoon, after she said goodbye to Bobby and his friend.

She'd finished her shift without writing up the verbal warning she'd handed out. It wasn't a requirement and fielding the inevitable questions was something she wanted to avoid. It wouldn't take long for the news to spread that the hometown hero really was back in town, but she wasn't going to be the one to herald Bobby's arrival.

Instead she offered quick goodbyes and walked out of the sheriff's office for the last time with the contents of her locker in a box, including the card she'd found wedged into the metal latch of the locker door, signed by everyone in the department. That was a nice surprise considering she'd refused the goodbye potluck dinner they'd wanted to throw for her.

Of course, tonight she had plans to meet up with Maggie and Racy at the Blue Creek Saloon, for her official "turning the page" party. Seeing how the next chapter in her life was nothing but a blank slate, Leeann didn't really feel like celebrating.

She wasn't worried about her lack of income despite the devastating loss of her inheritance and model earnings thanks to a Ponzi scheme a couple of years ago.

She still had enough money in the bank thanks to the sale of the land to pay the bills for a while, but her aunt's last round of cancer treatments had eaten up most of it. Thankfully, Ursula's latest medical checkup had come back negative and she was already back to work at her hair salon, but that still didn't explain the restlessness Leeann had been feeling for the past week.

Heck, for the past month. The past few months.

A restlessness that came to fruition this morning when—for the first time in a long time—she'd awakened without a plan.

Leeann always had a plan.

Most times in writing, sometimes only in her head. Knowing how her day was laid out—hour by hour, step by step—helped her to maintain balance and purpose for her life.

The last time she'd been without a plan had been thanks to a police investigation that came to an abrupt end with the decision there hadn't been enough evidence to go forward.

A decision that had reduced her to being a prisoner in her penthouse apartment in the heart of Manhattan. Rarely bothering to shower or get out of her pajamas, she'd had all her food delivered to her front door, her only contact with the outside world via her computer.

She hadn't even answered her cell phone, blessedly silent for weeks thanks to the press of a button. Not that she'd let that stop her from smashing it into a million confettilike pieces one night with a hammer—

"Stop!"

She jerked upright, her voice echoing in the quiet morning, bouncing off the water and causing her to blink.

She'd almost done it. She'd almost gotten

sucked back into the nightmare that had been her life six years ago. A nightmare she hadn't thought about for a very long time.

No, that's not true.

Three months ago she, Racy and Maggie had gone away for a girls' weekend at a spa in Jackson Hole. After a day filled with massages, facials and body wraps and a couple shared bottles of wine later by the fire, she'd finally disclosed to her best friends in the world her deepest secret.

Telling them hadn't been as hard as she'd thought it would be. They were very sweet and supportive, and Leeann now realized the restlessness she'd been feeling had started after that trip, despite her believing she'd truly moved on from the past.

Until last night.

Until Bobby had come back to town.

"Don't blame him. Your thoughts are your own. Your actions are your own." She spoke aloud her familiar mantra while dropping into a deep lunging stretch. Planting her hands midthigh, she lowered her forehead to her knee. "Your decisions are you own."

"Words to live by."

Chapter Three

The male voice caused Leeann to jerk upright; the sudden movement sent her stumbling backward. She lost her balance and ended up on her backside in the damp grass.

"Jeez, me and my big mouth." Bobby made his way toward her, leaning heavily on a cane. "Here, let me help—"

"Stop." Leeann scrambled to her feet, holding out one hand. "I'm up. I'm fine. I don't need your help."

Bobby slowed but continued walking. "Are you okay? I didn't mean to scare you."

"You didn't."

Conscious of her bare arms and abs thanks to the cropped tank top she wore that was nothing more than a fancy sports bra, Leeann moved past him to grab her jacket and yank it on. "What are you doing down here?"

He faced her. "I could ask you the same thing."

She righted her ball cap without removing it, but still met his gaze. "I own this land."

"And I own the road you used to get to this land."

Leeann tried not to stare as Bobby leaned slightly to his left, obviously favoring one leg as he gripped the carved head of his cane. Something he hadn't used yesterday when she'd ordered him out of his camper. "How did you even know I was—wait, you have a security system."

"Does that surprise you?"

No, it didn't. Not with the multimillion-dollar home he had built on the land adjacent to hers.

"There isn't an access road from the main highway to the pond," she explained. "I used your driveway, but I turned off just before the gate."

"Yeah, I saw the images."

This had to have been less than fifteen minutes ago.

Then he'd come here, using the path only the two of them had known about, the path she'd used all those years ago when she'd lived in a big house up on that same hill.

Memories of the times the two of them spent here together rushed back to her. Times they shrieked with laughter while splashing around in the icy water on a hot summer day, when she'd helped him understand the complexity of calculus, or the many times he'd held her close as she cried over yet another fight with her mother.

The time they'd fumbled through the unknown yet passion-filled moments of making love for the first time in a sleeping bag beneath a star-filled sky.

Leeann forced herself back to the present. She and Bobby were strangers to each other now.

"What are you thinking about?" He leaned forward, his gaze roaming from her head to her toes.

Just like he'd done yesterday. And like yesterday, her body responded with a heated flush she quickly blamed on her run.

"What—nothing." She took another step backward, an automatic reaction she had drilled into her head whenever anyone invaded her physical space.

"You do realize your face still gives away your thoughts?"

Only with him.

She'd learned over the years, first with her parents and then in New York, how to put on a false face, to pretend an emotion that didn't exist. Then later, she'd used that same skill at the police academy to prove to her instructors and fellow cadets she was more than just her looks.

Even here in Destiny among her former co-workers and friends, she worked hard to earn a reputation for having unflappable composure.

"I don't know what you're talking about." She pulled the brim of her cap lower over her eyes and turned away, her gaze on the still waters of her pond.

"Why'd you cut your hair?"

His simple question had her spinning back to look at him. The sun on his face made it hard for her to see his eyes. Was he laughing at her?

"I think that's why it took me so long to recognize you yesterday, that and the uniform." Bobby switched his cane from one hand to the other. "You always vowed you'd never cut your hair. Was it because of your job?"

"Huh?"

"Were you required to cut it when you became a cop?"

Dull kitchen scissors. Piles of knotted and tangled unwashed hair littering her lap and the gleaming hardwood floor beneath her. Frantic pounding on the door. Loud clicks of the locks releasing. The shock on her aunt's face when she found her sitting there—

Years of practice allowed her to shut down the memory.

"A deputy sheriff—" she corrected him, her voice barely a whisper. Pulling in a deep breath, she cleared her throat and answered his question. "And no, I cut my hair long before I went to the police academy."

"After you up and disappeared from your glamorous life in New York?"

He knew about that? Not that her career in high fashion was a secret, nor was her sudden retirement.

At one time she'd been one of the highest-paid models on the circuit with either her face or body gracing a different magazine every month. She'd split her time between New York, Paris and Milan, walking more than a million miles on the runway and posing for a hundred different shots in the quest for the perfect angle, the perfect composition, until that one day when she'd been too perfect and paid a horrible price.

Bobby tilted his head to one side and Leeann

realized he was waiting for an answer. "What was your question?"

"Did you cut your hair after you left New York?"

Technically, no, but thanks to her aunt she'd left the city the same night she'd hacked off the horrific reminder of what that maniac had done—

"Yes."

"So…" He dragged out the word, and tilted his head in the other direction. "How long have you been deputy sheriff?"

"Three years."

Bobby sighed. "You know, this would go a lot better if you gave me more than one- or two-word answers."

Crossing her arms over her chest was a purely defensive move, but she did it anyway. "What would?"

"Catching up. Getting to know each other again. It has been a few years since we've talked."

Fourteen years to be exact, but between the memories and his cutting remark from yesterday, she was quickly turning into a swirling mass of hurt and confusion, and she hated that. "Funny, I was under the impression you're not interested in anything I have to say."

That shut him up.

"What? No quick comeback?" She dropped her arms, suddenly very tired. "You didn't seem to have a problem putting me in my place yesterday. You must be losing your touch."

"I'm sorry, Lee." Bobby ran his fingers through his hair, pushing the dark strands off his face. He swayed for a moment, but adjusted his stance and kept talking. "I was a jerk and I can't even give you a good reason why. Zip and I had been on the road for over a week. I was in pain from sitting for twelve hours, pushing us to get here. Then of all the people to run into, barely over the county line…hell, maybe I am trying to give you a reason."

His quiet words surprised her, causing Leeann

to look at him, really look at him, seeing for the first time the tension in the lines around his mouth, the stiffness in his upper body.

It was evident he'd lost weight since his accident, but dressed in dark jeans and a black, short-sleeved collared shirt with his racing logo over his heart, he looked every inch the rich and famous stock car driver/celebrity/commercial spokesman he was.

Only at this moment he wasn't any of those things.

He was Bobby Winslow.

A boy who'd been her friend, her first love. And at one time, the most important person in her entire world.

"I'm sorry, too." The words fell from her lips, and the pain in her chest she'd blamed on her run eased. "I didn't expect—even with the house and all the rumors—I think I was as surprised to see you yesterday as you were to see me."

His mouth rose into his familiar grin that

always brought a devilish glint to his eyes. "So, is this a truce?"

"How about we just start over?"

"Sounds good to me." He stuck out one hand. "Hi. I'm Bobby Winslow."

Leeann stared at his tanned skin and long fingers. She'd bet his palm would still hold the same familiar calloused feel that spoke of years of hard work and manual labor.

It wasn't as if she avoided all human contact since—well, it wasn't, but over the years she'd cultivated a natural evasion to being touched.

Her fingers tingled at the prospect, but she shoved her hands into her jacket pockets. "Ah, I don't think we need to go back that far."

"Okay." Bobby dropped his hand and turned to look out over the pond. "You know, I thought about this place a lot over the years. Nice to know it's still as beautiful as ever."

"That's why I couldn't part with it."

He glanced at her, but then focused again on the water. "I'm sorry about your folks."

"Thanks, but that was a long—" She paused, the carefully segregated memories of her parents' death in a car accident and the horrific events of six months later tried to unite, but she mentally severed the connection and continued, "A long time ago."

"Your Aunt Ursula's still in town, right? Got her fingers in everyone's business as well as their hair?"

Leeann smiled. "Yes, she still has her beauty shop."

"I always liked her. It must've been nice to have her around after the fire," Bobby said. "You know, I was surprised when I found out you'd finally put the house and land up for sale. It stood empty for so long."

"I guess that makes us even," she said. "I was surprised when I found out the company buying it, B.W.I., stood for Bobby Winslow Incorporated."

"And yet you went through with the sale."

She'd had to no matter who the new owner

was, but it wasn't her place to share the reason. "The final papers had been signed by the time I found out."

"Meaning you wouldn't have gone through with it if you'd known I was the buyer?"

Would she have backed out? Leeann honestly didn't know the answer to that question.

"Do you plan to build your own place here?" he asked, filling the silence.

Making them neighbors? The words hung unspoken in the air.

Leeann shook her head. "No, I never thought about that. As you know, there isn't even an access road to this place. Besides, I like my house in town."

"Yeah, I never knew you and Mom lived on the same street."

Bobby moved beside her and even through her windbreaker, she could feel the natural warmth radiating off his body. Trapped between him and the water's edge, Leeann inched closer to the water, her sneakers sinking into the mud as she put more space between them. "I guess we keep on surprising each other. Like the fact Val wasn't with you yesterday."

"She was so supportive after my accident, never leaving my side, always encouraging me." He paused, then smiled. "Or kicking my butt, whichever tactic I needed at any given moment. Once I knew I was being released from rehab, I sent her and Paula, the head nurse who'd been assigned to my care for the last few months, on a three-week European cruise."

"I'm surprised she agreed to go. Val was so worried about you. I found her in her driveway, close to tears and unable to even lift her suitcase into the truck of her car." Leeann kicked at a rock, watching it plop into the water. "Once I calmed her down, I took her to the airport. I even promised I'd keep an eye on her garden while she was gone. Of course, neither of us knew she would be gone this long…"

Leeann realized Bobby had stopped walking.

She turned to look at him and saw an emotion on his face she couldn't read.

"Have you?" he asked.

"Have I what?"

"Taken care of her garden?"

Leeann smiled. "Of course. I weeded and watered, cut the flowers and harvested the veggies. Pretty soon I'll be getting it all tucked in for winter, but maybe your mom will be back before then."

"She said she had someone—a friend—taking care of her precious flowers, I never thought—"

"It could be me? I guess you didn't know we had become friends after I moved back to Destiny."

Bobby shook his head.

"Your mom was nice to me from the very start. It took a couple of weeks, but I finally worked up the courage to remind her who I was, which of course, she already knew. I never had a problem with your mom back when we—well, not that we spent a lot of time with her back then. It was my parents who hated the idea of us…spending time together."

"Believe me, my mom wasn't happy about you and me either. She just wasn't as vocal about it."

"She was afraid the town's princess was going to hurt you."

Bobby shrugged, but Leeann could see the truth in his eyes.

"And I did just as she feared."

"It was a long time ago." Bobby used his cane to point toward the old path. "So, what do you think of my house?"

"I've never seen it."

"Really? The Murphys told me the construction site was a regular tourist attraction until the security system went live."

"Yes, the local paper ran a weekly report of what was happening up here."

"And you weren't curious at all?"

She had been. Often when she spent time here at the pond, she could hear the low rumble of construction equipment and men talking to each other as they worked, but something always kept her from going to check the building out.

A surprise considering Leeann had never liked her former home here.

Her mother, a transplanted Southern belle, had designed the two-story Georgian mansion, complete with tall white columns that looked out of place in this majestic wooded setting.

Plus a complicated pregnancy had resulted in Leeann being an only child, making her a constant reminder of why only two of the home's six bedrooms had been filled.

Her life had changed so much since she'd broken free of the gilded cage, it'd almost been a relief when a fire had made the house uninhabitable, then the quick sale—

"Do you want to come take a look?"

His softly spoken question caused Leeann to focus on the ground to keep Bobby from seeing her face beneath the brim of her cap. "Oh, no, I should be heading back to town."

"Are you working today?"

"No, I'm—" A rumbling from Leeann's stomach stopped her words. She slapped her hands over her midsection.

Bobby offered a light chuckle, then said, "Come on, I'll even feed you."

Leeann looked at him and saw his familiar smile again, more relaxed now. A throwback to his rogue rebel days. Before she knew it, they were at the path she hadn't used since selling the land.

"Ladies first."

The ground was smoother here and more defined, but it still must've been hard for Bobby to get down to the pond, especially on a cane. "Why don't you go first?"

"I can handle the climb, Lee. I don't need you to play rescuer if I take a tumble."

"You've only been out of rehab a few days."

He raised one eyebrow in a quizzical glance.

"Yesterday's headlines were about you." She quickly filled him in on the front-page article.

"They even had a picture of you in a wheelchair."

A shadow passed over his eyes, then it was gone. He swung the cane easily in front of him. "No worries. I've been walking on my own since the middle of July. I only use this on occasion."

Leeann didn't want to argue so she started up the dirt path, conscious of his gaze on her backside the entire way. When they reached the clearing, she paused, amazed at the scattering of log buildings, including a huge log barn with a red metal roof.

"Wow, that barn is amazing."

"I replaced the original structure, which was in terrible condition, and matched the style of the other buildings," Bobby said, joining her.

"Well, you've built more than just a house it seems. You've got your own compound." She kept her gaze forward, but her peripheral vision allowed her to see the exertion on Bobby's face. His slow, deep breaths told her the climb had been harder on him than he'd let on. "What are you going to do with all those buildings?"

"Some are for storage," Bobby pointed out as he kept walking. "The remaining are empty, but they can be used as staff—ah, guest quarters."

She followed his lead and they crossed the clearing. Leeann climbed into the passenger side of what looked like a souped-up golf cart with all-terrain tires and a cargo box on the back.

Bobby slid behind the wheel and soon he was maneuvering the vehicle along the freshly paved road, its twists and turns so familiar to her, laid out so because her mother hadn't wanted to see the old barn from her front porch.

"The new barn will hold eight horses total. I've got three coming up from a farm in North Carolina in the next month or so, before winter sets in," Bobby said. "I recently bought two more from a ranch in Texas called Still Waters, but they won't be here until next spring."

The name of the ranch caught her by surprise. "That's Landon's ranch."

"Landon Cartwright, right?"

"How did you know that?"

"I dealt with a Chase Cartwright down in Texas," Bobby said. "When I told him where I needed the horses sent, he mentioned his brother lived up here."

"Landon is married to Maggie Stevens—do you remember Maggie?" Bobby nodded, so she continued, "Anyway, they married a year ago and run The Crescent Moon ranch here in Destiny, together, but he's still involved with his family's ranch in Texas, too."

"Talk about a small world. I plan to talk to Maggie about getting even more horses from her place."

Leeann had read enough about Bobby's career over the past few years to know his entire racing operation was based in North Carolina. Having horses seemed to suggest his stay would be permanent, unless of course, he planned to have a staff to take care of them, and in turn, take care of his house.

Last night she'd finally nodded off convinced Bobby was only back in town temporarily as he continued recovering from his accident. She knew they were bound to run into each other again while he was here, she just hadn't expected it to be as soon as today.

But after clearing the air back at the pond, they were talking and acting like adults who allowed their shared history to stay where it belonged.

In the past.

Would that change if he—

"Are you planning on sticking around?" The words fell from her mouth before she could stop them. "I'm so sorry," she hastily added, "that was rude. It's really none of my business."

Was it none of her business?

Up until an hour ago, Bobby would've agreed with her. He would've made it clear that despite building his dream home, he hadn't planned to reside in Destiny full-time, even though the thought of moving back home had crossed his mind a few times during his rehabilitation. He knew his mom wanted him here. No matter how many times he'd tried to convince her to move south to live closer to him, she'd refused.

If pressed, he'd have to admit he'd purchased the land and built the house just because all this once belonged to Leeann's parents.

Then he'd come up with the idea of creating new headquarters for his racing organization. A place complete with a regulation-size test track, now that he had all the room he needed right here on his land.

Of course, all of that had been before he'd found out Leeann was back in town.

Did that changed everything?

He had no idea.

Silence stretched between them as Bobby eased the cart around the circular drive, passing the garage to the left, two bays on either side of a covered pull through that led to the main road.

He slowed to a stop, shut off the engine and stared straight ahead, his hands gripping the steering wheel. "Would that be so bad? Me sticking around?"

When she didn't answer him, he turned to her. She had slid out of the passenger side of the utility cart and was standing there, staring up at his home.

He joined her, a shot of pure pleasure racing through his veins at the stunned expression on her face. Unable to see her eyes from beneath that ball cap she wore, he found his gaze locked on her mouth and the way her plump, pink lips parted.

He wanted to kiss her.

Right here. Right now.

Forget the fourteen years that separated them, forget the way she'd destroyed his dreams, forget all he'd accomplished in order to prove to everyone, to her, that there was more to Bobby Winslow than they'd ever known.

He pulled in a deep breath, bringing with it the clean, biting scent of the forest of trees surrounding them, the warm sun and the woman standing next to him.

A powerful need filled him, a need to hold her in his arms, to feel the tightly toned body he'd gotten a glimpse of earlier before she'd hid it beneath her jacket…

"Oh, Bobby."

Her words came out in a reverent whisper and he had to grip the cane with two hands to stop himself from acting on an impulse he was sure was only one-sided.

"I can't even put it into words…I can't describe…"

She turned to him, having to tip her head back as he stood so close. Now he could see her eyes. They widened, the hazel coloring that always looked more golden than green flashing at him as their gazes locked and held.

What did she see when she looked at him?

The rebellious punk he'd been as a kid, always breaking the rules, with a white-hot temper his mother said came from his wayward father?

Or did she see the successful businessman he'd become?

A man who'd left the army after serving honorably for four years and then worked his way up through the ranks to become one of the best drivers in the America's Cup Pro Racing circuit. A spokesperson that promoted more products than Jeff Gordon and Shaquille O'Neal and appeared in more print ads and commercials than all the Kardashian sisters combined.

A man who accomplished all he'd vowed to do.

"Yes, it is beautiful…and mine. Finally, I'm allowed inside. And unlike the way your parents treated me, you're welcome in my home anytime."

Chapter Four

Bobby expected his declaration to bring a flash of anger to Leeann's eyes. Instead sadness and regret reflected in those green-golden depths, a testament to how she knew the way her parents had treated him was unjust.

Warm breath rushed from between her lips and brushed over his. His gaze lowered to her mouth and he dipped his head.

Leeann blinked and scurried backward until she bumped into the front tire of the cart.

She grabbed on to the vehicle's metal framework to steady herself, looking around at his house, the surrounding trees, the driveway with its stone sculpture surrounded by flowers in the center.

Anywhere but on him.

And wasn't that a kick in the gut.

But a well-needed one.

Getting caught up in the past—their past—was the last thing he needed right now. Just because they'd managed to be civil to each other for the past thirty minutes didn't mean either of them wanted—

Ah, hell, he wanted and she obviously didn't.

Bobby straightened and moved toward his house. Legs stiff from standing too long in one spot, he stumbled, but caught himself with the cane, hoping he kept it from being noticeable.

Thankfully, he felt no tremors as he stepped onto the covered porch bracketed by two columns of stacked river rocks on either end. He pushed open one side of the heavy double entrance doors before facing her. "After you."

She stared at him for a moment, and he wondered if she was going to turn and run, literally. Then she dropped her shoulders and angled her head just a touch off center, a move so familiar from their childhood whenever anyone challenged her, he had to bite back a grin.

Walking—gliding—onto the porch, she moved past him with the grace that spoke of her years on pageant stages and modeling runways.

"This is the foyer, obviously," Bobby said, closing the door behind him. "And straight ahead is the great room."

Leeann paused in front of the two-sided wood-burning fireplace on a raised hearth that served as a divider between the two areas. He wished he'd thought to hit the auto ignition switch for the fireplace when he'd first opened the door so she could get the full effect.

He stood next to her, but she scooted away and walked into the room. Following her, he watched as she took in the custom-designed leather furniture, rustic wrought-iron tables and priceless artwork scattered around the room before she looked upward.

"The vaulted ceilings are over twenty feet high and those are hammered beam trusses," he said. "They start back at the entry and run the entire length of the room and out onto the deck."

"Well, when you said impressive, you meant it. Looks like it came right out of *Luxury Homes of the Rich and Famous.*"

Zip had pretty much said the same thing this morning. So why did it bother him more coming from Leeann? "I wasn't about to move into an empty space. Having my home ready when I got here was important—"

He was interrupted by barking that started in the distance but quickly grew in volume. The sounds of doggy nails on the hardwood floors announced Daisy's arrival. She skidded to a stop at Bobby's feet, catching him at midcalf with her forehead.

Ah, damn! Bobby gripped the cane with two

hands and locked his knees. "Thanks a lot, Daiz."

"Come back here, you crazy mutt," Zip called out, rounding the corner that led from the kitchen and adjoining family room. "It's just Ace, and it's about time. I was getting worried. Hey! If it isn't my favorite cop."

Leeann offered an easy grin. "And just how many cops do you know, Mr. Zippenella?"

Zip offered one of his lady-killer smiles. Bobby wanted to cross the room and give the guy a quick cuff to the back of his head.

"Not counting two of my sisters, three uncles and my pop?" Zip spoke over the dog's contin- ued barking. "And what's with this mister stuff? Call me Dean—okay, Daisy, knock it off!"

She left Bobby's side, making a beeline for her master, but continued with a vocal assault directed at Leeann so strong it had the dog's hind legs kicking up off the ground.

"Oh, I'm not going to hurt you," Leeann cooed,

dropping to a crouch and holding out her hand toward Daisy. "Come here, come say hi."

"Whoa, you shouldn't—"

"Lee, don't." Bobby's command overrode Zip's as he hurried across the room.

She slowly withdrew her fingers and looked up at him, then to Zip and back to him. "What—why?"

"Daisy doesn't like females." Zip snapped his fingers to get his dog's attention. She finally obeyed and sat at his side, low growls vibrating deep in her throat, her shaggy coat standing on end in a straight line down her back.

"Really?" Leeann rose. "How come?"

"We don't know." Bobby stepped closer, moving in front of his best friend. "She's been that way ever since Zip found her."

"Let me get her out of here or she'll never stop." With one hand scooped under her belly, Zip easily picked up the dog and headed for one of the matching glass doors that led to the covered deck. "Daisy's still got lots of moxie for an old broad."

"Oh, no, please don't tie her up because of me."

"He's just going to put her outside," Bobby said.

"But she might run off."

"Naw, she's only gone out as far as the closest tree to pee behind." Zip plopped the dog down on the wooden surface and quickly closed the door.

Daisy whined, but stopped when Zip leveled a pointed finger in her direction. Instead, she started to pace back and forth, pausing at times to place one paw on the glass.

"I don't think my baby is a forest kind of girl," Zip continued. "She prefers the open beaches of the Jersey Shore. I guess sand's in her blood."

"So is mistrusting females," Leeann said. "Poor thing, she must've been hurt pretty bad by someone in her past."

"Yeah, well, a female will do that to ya." Zip

joined them again. "At least that's what I know from my limited experience."

Bobby rolled his eyes, wishing his buddy had gone outside along with Daisy. "Limited experience, my ass."

"Come on, now, bro. Don't be dissing me in front of our guest." Zip grinned. "So where did you two run into each other. Oh, wait, I get it now. The law is a trespasser."

"I wasn't trespassing," Leeann protested. "Well, not much."

"And as a reward the master of the house offered a tour of his humble abode."

Leeann looked around the room again, her gaze lingering on the signed Ansel Adams photograph hanging over the fireplace. As hard as he tried, Bobby couldn't get a read on what she really thought of his home.

"Humble, indeed," she said. "Plenty big enough for the two—ah, three of you, I guess."

"You haven't seen anything yet." Zip beckoned with a wave of one hand, backing through the archway behind him. "Come check out this killer kitchen."

Leeann walk into the adjoining room and Bobby was pleased to hear a catch in her breath as she came to a stop.

The furniture in there was more casual in design. Built-in cabinets lined the far wall; a flat-screen television, state-of-the-art stereo and video gaming system lay hidden behind the doors. Books and artwork, mainly his collection of Frederic Remington bronze sculptures, filled the open shelving. The other wall held an original, one-of-a-kind oil painting by contemporary cowboy artist Michael Swearingin that dominated the space with its sheer size.

"Oh, how wonderful!"

Bobby followed her, eager to see which piece had caught her eye, but Leeann had gone straight to the floor-to-ceiling glass windows that allowed a breathtaking view of the forest and Laramie Mountains outside.

She spun around, a wide smile on her face.

"This is so beautiful. What a view! Our kitchen used to be on this side of the house, but the windows never let in a sight like this!"

Leeann turned back to the scene and Bobby walked over to the bar that separated the open kitchen from the family room. He grabbed one of the water bottles Zip had taken from the refrigerator, ignoring his friend's pointed stare.

"Museum-quality fingerpaints and enough bronze to sink a battleship, and *that's* what impresses the lady?" Zip's voice was low as he twisted the cap off a bottle, replacing it with the still-closed one in Bobby's grip. "I like her."

"Yeah, big surprise."

"Take her a drink—she looks thirsty."

Crossing the room, Bobby joined Leeann, holding out the water. "Thought you might need this."

"Thanks, I do." She took the bottle and easily put a couple of feet between them as she faced the room. "I know I keep saying this, but again, pretty impressive."

Yeah, just like she kept moving away from him. "Let me show you the rest while Zip whips up something for lunch."

Leeann tipped the bottle to her lips for a quick sip while crossing the room, heading for the kitchen. "Don't tell me you're Bobby's personal chef?"

Zip let out a laugh and leaned against the counter. "Why? Don't I look like a chef?"

"Hmm, I think not. Maybe you're one of his mechanics?"

"Well, I keep his engine running, but it's more of a personal thing. I'm his physical therapist."

She turned back to look at Bobby.

He forced himself to stand perfectly still as her gaze traveled the length of his body, pausing on his cane, before she spoke.

"You have your own physical therapist?"

"Yes."

Silence filled the air as she stared at him. Bobby caught Zip shooting him a scowl from behind Leeann, a silent demand that he offer more of an explanation.

"We met a little over ten years ago while in the army," he finally said. "Zip was the medic in my unit and we usually ended up on patrol together. We spent a lot of time in the Middle East, be- tween official wars with fancy names like Desert Shield and Enduring Freedom, doing—well, doing our jobs."

"That's where I found Daisy. She followed us back to our base one day and stuck around," Zip added. "It took a bit of maneuvering, but I managed to get her back to the U.S. in one piece. Thanks to my boss I managed to do the same."

"Zip and I ended up leaving the army around the same time," Bobby interrupted, walking over to join them. "Went our separate ways but kept in touch. Zip continued working in the medical field, becoming a physical therapist, and I got into racing."

"And now you work for him?" Leeann asked, looking at Zip.

"As soon as I heard about Bobby's accident, Daisy and I hopped in my car and left the Garden State behind."

"After my mom, his ugly mug was the first thing I saw when I came out of the coma." Bobby propped a forearm against one of the leather and hardwood counter stools as the memory returned. He swallowed hard against the sudden dryness in his throat. "I couldn't feel anything from the waist down. Zip promised me I'd walk again. He was right."

"As long as he paid me to work my magic," Zip added with a grin, flexing his fingers. "So I quit my job, moved to North Carolina and five months later we're in his beautiful yet boring log castle here in Destiny, Wyoming."

"Speaking of my castle—" The ringing of his cell phone cut him off. Grabbing it from his pocket, he looked at the display. "Damn, I need to answer this."

"Oh, well." Leeann placed her half-empty water bottle on the counter. "I should be going anyway. I need to get down to the Youth Center in a couple of hours."

"This place is big, but the rest of the tour won't take that long." Zip slid around the counter. "I'll take over as your tour guide. We'll start with the two guest rooms on this side and then proceed to the lower level. Nothing else is interesting up here, just the master suite at the other end. But you've got to see the wet room."

"Wet room?" Confusion colored her voice as she glanced over her shoulder at Bobby.

"Yeah, you know, the sauna, hot tub, an indoor lap pool…" Zip's voice faded as he led Leeann away.

Bobby watched them go, pushing down the rush of panic that had filled him when she'd mentioned leaving. He had no idea where that had come from or why a perverse sense of satisfaction took its place as she deftly put space between herself and Zip.

Just like she'd done with him.

He took the call when his phone rang again,

knowing his business manager wouldn't stop trying until he reached him. "Hey, Jasper."

"So you made it to the Wild West in one piece?"

"We got in yesterday afternoon. I was planning on calling later today."

"This can't wait, Bobby. Rawhide Cologne heard you were out of rehab and they want to move up the photo shoot."

Now that he was alone, Bobby finally sat down on the stool, appreciating the chance to take his weight off his legs. "We've already talked about this. I'm concentrating on getting healthy. I don't want anything on my schedule for the foreseeable future, and that includes endorsement work. You said you got the okay from all the sponsors."

"I did, I did, but the parent company has decided to hold back the new commercial you shot before the accident for their men's bath product line until the football playoffs. Maybe even the Super Bowl."

Bobby sighed, wishing he hadn't agreed to

this contract. He never used the stuff, prefer-
ring nothing on his skin but soap and water, but
the money had been too good to pass up.

"They've offered to send a sizable check
to your favorite charity if you agree." Jasper
paused, letting that information sink in. "It's just
for a few hours and the same guy who shot the
commercial will do the stills. And they'll come
to you."

"Meaning what? Come to the house?"

"With the way you've done the place up, it
fits perfectly with the product!" The Southern
twang deepened in Jasper's voice, as it always
did whenever he was excited about an idea. "The
old West, the forgotten and lonely cowboy waiting on his lady love to return, then the image
morphs from black-and-white to color, the
modern cowboy still waiting on a lady..."

Bobby had to agree, remembering how the
commercial was shot partly in a ghost town in
the Dakota badlands. "Okay, but this is it, and

tell them to make that check out to that kid's camp, Victory Junction, in Randleman."

"Will do. The photographer and his team arrive in Cheyenne in a few days. They'll be at your place next Friday, around nine."

"That soon?"

"Yes. And remember, the more you cooperate the sooner it'll be over. Then you can go back to doing whatever it is you couldn't take care of in Carolina."

"Jas, I told you. I wanted to continue my re-cuperation here—"

"Yeah, yeah, I know. So, how are you feeling?"

Bobby honestly didn't know. Physically he was okay, even though he should probably sit with his feet up for the next couple of hours.

It was a different story when it came to what he was experiencing deep inside. He hadn't been this torn up emotionally for years, not since his return from his last tour overseas, a week before his honorable discharge.

Was it being back in his hometown? Or was it Leeann?

Not willing to go into any of that with the man who handled his business dealings, he instead assured Jasper he was fine and would check in with him next week. Ending the call, he pushed away from the bar, anxious to find Zip and Leeann.

His legs a bit shaky, he used the elevator he'd included in the home design, more in case his mother needed it someday, but a fateful decision considering the accident. Stepping out into the exercise room on the lower level, he didn't hear anything. Unusual because Zip rarely shut up unless he was asleep.

After a quick peek into the pool area, he walked into the rec room and found Leeann alone, standing in front of the display of awards, honors and promotional work he'd done over the years.

Most of the plaques and photos had been stored away in North Carolina, unseen by even him for years. When he'd given the design team permission to take anything from the waterfront condo he lived in for this place, he never thought they'd bring this stuff out here, much less create a floor-to-ceiling display.

Not that he wasn't proud of what he'd accomplished in his life. Damn straight he was. He'd worked hard for every one of those accolades, both on the racetrack and off.

He watched as she looked at the wall, arms crossed over her chest, that ball cap of hers making it hard to read the expression on her face.

Thick carpeting silenced his steps as he passed by twin couches and matching chairs that looked too comfortable. He headed instead for the pool table in front of the double doors that led to the lower-level outdoor patio. A wall of glass flooded this room with natural light. The two other bedrooms were down here—one of which Zip claimed last night—along with an adjoin-

CHRISTYNE BUTLER   103

ing room that held the full-size bar and another fireplace.

"So, what do you think?"

Leeann spun around. "Oh! I didn't hear you come in."

"I figured you might not hear me coming because Zip loves the sound of his own voice, but you're here all alone."

"Dean went to go check on Daisy."

He nodded. "I'm not surprised. Those two have quite a bond."

"So do the two of you, it seems."

"He's the brother I never had." Bobby hitched one hip on the edge of the table. "I know I wouldn't be standing here on my own two feet without him."

"And it's a pretty impressive place to be standing."

He faced her again. "That seems to be your favorite word when describing my home."

She looked around. "Well, it's…big."

His internal radar went on full alert. What

wasn't she saying? "Why don't you tell me what you really think?"

Leeann shrugged, still refusing to meet his eyes. "Your decorators did an amazing job."

"But?"

"But something about it is just too…"

"Too…" He prodded again when her voice trailed off. "Come on, Lee, we've known each other too long for you to be firewalling me like this."

"Excuse me?"

"Sorry, racing term. Just tell me what you think, okay?"

She raised one hand in a helpless gesture before letting it fall back to her side. "It's really more of an attraction than a home. Yes, all the artwork, expensive furniture and fixtures are beautiful, but it feels…lifeless." She turned back to the awards wall. "Like it's all just for show."

Her words caused a deep freeze low in his gut. "For show? As in showing off?"

"Look at all of these." She waved at the section of framed photographs. "You with the vice president, with George Clooney, with the Dallas Cowboy cheerleaders. Heck, this one has you sandwiched between Tom Brady and Gisele Bündchen."

"That was taken at their wedding. I was a guest."

"Of course you were." She again crossed her arms over her chest and took a step backward even though there was at least three feet between them already. "Destiny is a small town with real people living normal lives. They worry about keeping their jobs, paying their bills and finding a way to put their kids through college.

"But you know all that, Bobby, because you too once lived in this town. Back when you made a promise not to set foot in it again until you could return a big success with all the money in the world."

An icy wave coursed through him despite the warmth of the sun hitting his back through the glass doors. He remained silent and allowed her to speak, to throw his words back at him this time.

Yes, he'd said all that—and more—the day she'd told him she'd chosen a shot at the glamorous life of high-fashion modeling over being his teenage bride.

"What can I say?" His reply came out clipped and edgy, sharp as a shard of cut glass. "Mission accomplished."

"Yes, so it seems." She pressed the fingers of one hand against her lips, as if she was stopping herself from saying anything more. "It's probably best if I go now. Don't worry, I can show myself out."

And just like that, Leeann Harris walked out on him.

Again.

Chapter Five

"And then the great Bobby Winslow walked into the Youth Center and the kids went nuts." Leeann crushed another shell between her fingers. Digging out the peanuts, she tossed them into her mouth and chased them down with a healthy swallow of frozen margarita.

She was babbling. Unusual for her, but she couldn't stop.

The way she'd talked to Bobby this morning, in his own home no less, still made her cringe. Even as the words had flowed from her mouth, she couldn't believe what she'd heard herself saying.

He'd invited her into his house and what had she done? Torn him up one side and down the other for making a hard-won success of his life.

Would she feel better if he'd turned out to be a bum?

Her two best friends sat across from her in one of the circular booths at the Blue Creek Saloon, a legendary bar in Destiny, and had let her blather nonstop since they'd arrived a half hour ago. She'd told them everything, from the surprising reunion yesterday on the side of the road, to her mouthy critique of his log mansion, to his surprise appearance this afternoon during her volunteer stint at the Youth Center.

"Can you believe that? Then before he leaves he pulls out his checkbook and just like that—" she snapped her fingers "—we have the cash to take the teens on the previously-canceled-for-lack-of-funds ski trip scheduled for the Christmas holidays."

A deep breath, another chug on her margarita, then one more deep breath, this time released with an audible sigh that signaled she was done.

Finally.

Eyeing Racy and Maggie, her confidants since grade school, she waited for them to agree with her.

"Boy, what a jerk." Racy Steele tried but failed to hide her grin behind her glass of iced tea. "I'll have Gage lock him up the next time he dares show his face in town."

"Oh, I totally agree," Maggie Cartwright added, cracking open a peanut shell for herself. "One hundred percent, grade-A slime."

"Sorry I'm late." Gina Steele, Racy's sister-in-law, slid into the booth next to Leeann. "Justin and I had a heck of a time finding the video Jacoby wanted to take with him on his sleepover with Anna. I swear that little boy is as messy as his father, but I've got to tell you, Maggie, he is so excited about spending time out at your ranch with your little girl. So, what'd I miss? Who's slime?"

"Bobby Winslow," Racy and Maggie said in unison.

Gina blinked. "Bobby 'Sexy as Sin, Sweet as Candy' Winslow? Hometown hero and stock car driver extraordinaire?"

"Hey, don't let my brother hear you talking like that," Racy said, then grinned. "Justin might get jealous."

"I'm taken, not dead," Gina shot back. "And if you all can look at Bobby's Wrangler-encased butt and not sigh, then you're stronger than me."

"He probably wears Wranglers because he gets paid to," Leeann said.

"So?" Gina replied. "I guess the female population of Destiny will just have to suffer with the hardship of a great-looking backside."

"Speaking of backsides…" Maggie paused, a twinkle in her blue eyes. "Check out the cowboys at the end of the main bar."

Gina and Racy immediately did as Maggie

requested, but Leeann resisted. Or at least she tried to.

She knew what she would see.

She didn't know how, but she did.

Bobby was here.

Unable to stand it any longer, she turned and scoped out the area, easily locating the group of men through the growing crowd. Even from the back she identified Landon, Maggie's husband, the only true cowboy in the bunch.

Next to him stood Gage, Racy's husband and Gina's brother, and as the sheriff of Destiny, Leeann's former boss. Also with them was Racy's brother, Justin Dillon, who happened to be Gina's fiancé, even if she still wore the engagement ring he'd given her last spring on her right hand rather than her left.

Walking up to join them with hearty handshakes and a few backslaps was Bobby. He looked right at home in his jeans, boots, brushed cotton shirt and Stetson. He was doing without the cane he'd clung to earlier today. He greeted the bartenders and shook a few hands before grabbing an offered beer.

Damn. Leeann had to admit that he did indeed fill out his Wranglers to perfection.

"Hey, who's that walking wall of muscles behind Bobby?" Gina asked.

Wearing a T-shirt that hugged his massive arms and chest and a battered Mets cap instead of a Stetson, Dean fit right in. He quickly took the beer Bobby held out and soon shook hands with the others when introductions were made.

"Jeez, he must be Winslow's bodyguard," Racy said. "Look at the size of those shoulders."

"That's Zippy—I mean, Dean Zippenella. I met him when I pulled them over yesterday. He's Bobby's…friend." So why did she feel the need to protect Bobby's privacy all of a sudden?

Turning back around, Leeann waved down their passing waitress, more than ready to order another round. Margaritas for her, Maggie and Gina, and an iced tea for Racy, who at only four months pregnant looked as big as a house.

Still, she was a beautiful, glowing image of motherhood.

"'Ritas all around and another iced tea for your boss," she said to Becky, a waitress who Racy, as the owner of the Blue Creek, had recently hired. "I'll make it easy for you, all frozen, all with salt."

"Ah, no, not for me." Maggie waved a hand at Becky. "I'll just take another ice water."

"Hey, we're supposed to be celebrating tonight." Gina reached for a handful of peanuts from the bowl in the center of the table, then gestured over one shoulder. "Didn't you tell your hubby he's the designated driver?"

An angelic smile came over Maggie's face, a perfect match to her wavy golden hair. "That was the plan, yes, but…things changed this afternoon at the doctor's. I'm pregnant."

Silence filled the air for a long moment, then peanuts went flying as the table erupted with shouts of joy, hand clapping and hugs.

Leeann's gaze instinctively went to Bobby at

Maggie's announcement, then jerked away as she scooted across the space and wrapped her friend in a strong hug.

"I'm so happy for you," she whispered in her friend's ear, blaming the sting in her eyes on Maggie's curls in her face.

"Thanks, sweetie, I know you are." Maggie pulled back, her gaze sharp as she caught Leeann's. "Are you all right?"

"Yes, I'm fine." She brushed her hair back from her face, using the moment to wipe the wetness from her eyes. "This is so exciting. I know how much you wanted Anna to grow up with brothers and sisters."

"How far along are you?" Racy gave Maggie's hand a squeeze. "Did they give you a due date?"

"April of next year."

"Just a couple of months after me." Racy caressed her swollen belly. "The babies will love having a playmate so close in age."

"Yeah, imagine us pregnant at the same—wait

a minute." Maggie's eyes grew round. "Did you say *babies?*"

Racy nodded, her smile wide. "Being this big at four months isn't just because of the Blue Creek Burger, extra pickles and special sauce that I can't seem to get enough of. Gage and I are expecting twins."

More excited squeals, especially from Gina, who Leeann guessed was hearing the news about being an aunt twice over for the first time by the way she jumped from her seat to hug her sister-in-law.

"Does all this family expansion give you any ideas?" Racy returned Gina's eager embrace. "Not that I'm pushing you in the baby department, but helping you plan a spring wedding would certainly keep my mind off stretch marks and swollen ankles."

"Justin and I are busy with work, both of us getting our teaching credentials and raising Jacoby." Gina smiled as she took her seat again, looking at her ring. "That's more than enough plans for our future, for the moment anyway. Besides, planning a nursery for two babies with plenty of input from my mom, is going to keep you very busy."

Their drinks arrived and Leeann quickly grabbed hers. She didn't know why, but she felt like a total loser compared to her friends, who all faced their futures with such purpose and happiness.

Leeann, on the other hand, didn't have any plans for what she was going to do tomorrow, the next six months or even next spring. And like earlier, not having a reason to get out of bed in the morning, other than to run, burned a hole in her gut. A fire she was determined to extinguish in tequila, triple sec and lime.

"The way you're tossing back that drink, I'm guessing you're not driving tonight."

Leeann froze, the salt from her glass burning her upper lip as Bobby's voice poured over her shoulder. She took another swallow, barely holding back a gag as a splash of booze went down too fast. Placing her drink on the table with a loud thud, she noticed the guys had joined them while she was hosting her internal pity party.

Landon and Gage had moved in behind their wives, elbows resting on the back of the booth, while Dean now sat in the empty spot next to her, Gina and Justin having disappeared to the dance floor. That left Bobby standing behind her in the space between their booth and the next one.

"No—" She coughed, not turning to look at him as she finally answered, "No, I'm not driving."

"Hey you, how's it going?" Dean leaned toward her, but before he could bump her shoulder with his, Leeann scooted farther inward, squashing the panic that automatically rose.

When would she ever get over that?

"Ah, good, it's good." She forced the words from her throat as she waved at her girlfriends. "Have you met everyone?"

More introductions were made with Dean

taking some good-natured ribbing about his accent. He assured them he was enjoying Wyoming, but while one could take the boy out of Jersey, it was darn near impossible to take Jersey out of the boy.

Racy and Maggie peppered him with questions, asking if the MTV reality show was anything like real life, and Leeann found herself relaxing a bit as Dean shared stories of growing up in Point Pleasant Beach on the Jersey Shore.

Suddenly, warm heat brushed against her right shoulder. Her breath caught, then disappeared entirely when that heat moved from her shoulder to her elbow and down the long sleeve covering her skin. She froze, tightening her grip on her glass, and resisted the urge to crush her arms to her sides in an attempt to make herself as small as possible.

Bobby set the empty beer bottle on the table next to her margarita glass. His head was so close to hers as he leaned over the back of the booth she could feel the brim of his Stetson brushing her hair.

"Do you mind if I put this here?" he asked, his words slightly raspy.

She shook her head, mortified she couldn't find the strength to put voice to words. She saw Racy and Maggie watching her, concern in their eyes. She offered a quick wiggle of her fingers, hoping it conveyed that she was okay.

But she wasn't okay because her fingers unwittingly swept over his. Her heart raced and she couldn't tell if that was a good thing or not. Learned behavior dictated that she maintain distance between herself and—well, everyone, but now Bobby's hand was a hairbreadth away from hers.

"So, did you see our homage to you and your racing career when you walked into the lobby, Bobby?" Racy asked. "Everyone in Destiny is so proud of all you've accomplished."

"Not everyone."

His whispered words, meant for Leeann's ears

only, rushed hot against her skin as he straightened and drew his hand away. Leeann released her glass and tucked her hair behind one ear, surprised she didn't find the smooth locks on fire from the heat of Bobby's gaze on the back of her head. She straightened her shoulders, but when she bumped up against his hands resting on the back of the booth, she instinctively leaned forward.

"Yes, I noticed the display," he continued. "It's not necessary, but thanks. What I liked even more was the wall honoring the residents who are serving in the military with their unit flags and insignias. There must be at least two dozen photographs hanging there."

"Between those on active duty and the ones serving with the National Guard units, we've got quite a few people overseas," Gage said. "We've lost a couple, too, including Scott Coggen, just this past summer. He was with the Air National Guard out of Cheyenne. I don't know if you remember him? He was a few years ahead of you in school."

"The name sounds familiar."

"His wife—well, his widow, Fay, is the local florist," Maggie added. "They owned Fay's Flowers on Main Street."

"I remember hearing about his funeral. Mom often read the local paper online while she was with me in the hospital."

"You know, you do look pretty good for someone who—well, for—I mean, that was a hell of a crash back in May," Landon observed. "Hope you don't mind me pointing out the obvious."

"No, I don't mind. It was pretty impressive."

"That's one way of describing it," Dean added, his fingers busy peeling the label on his beer bottle.

Leeann would use another word.

Horrific.

The first photo of the crash had captured Bobby's car in midair, him still behind the wheel, the front end a twisted mess of crushed metal and the hood flying free overhead.

Of course, the news and the internet allowed people to watch a video of what happened next, the car flipping end over end a half-dozen times before it came to a stop upside down with Bobby's prone body lying motionless on the grass beside it.

Leeann's fingers tightened around the stem of her glass.

She remembered walking into the break room at the sheriff's office to find her coworkers huddled around the television the morning of the crash. She'd stayed and watched the video because she knew everyone expected her to walk away. It'd taken all her strength to maintain her well-known, unflappable expression with the eyes of the entire room upon her.

Later, alone at home laying in the dark, she'd watched it again, just to prove to herself she could. It'd taken a week of daily five-mile runs to ease the stone-cold ache in her gut.

That and the news he was going to survive.

"It wasn't too much fun from inside the car either." Bobby's rough voice cut through her thoughts as he paused to clear his throat. "I'm not back one hundred percent yet, but I'm very lucky."

"Speaking of lucky." Dean tilted his bottle to his lips and drained the last of his beer. "How do I find someone willing to show me the fine art of two-stepping?"

Moments later, Dean was in the arms of a bubbly blonde with Maggie and Landon joining them on the dance floor. That left Racy, Gage, Bobby and her at the table. Soon people started to flock around their booth once they realized the hometown hero was there.

Leeann slid out of the seat, refusing to be blocked in.

Except Bobby managed to do just that by moving from behind the booth to stand next to her.

With one hand braced on the seat's edge,

he caged her between him and the table as he smiled and talked, catching up with old friends from high school and meeting new people who'd moved into town since he'd been gone.

He handed out autographs when asked, glossing over any details of the accident as if he'd merely run a red light or had a flat tire.

She couldn't believe it.

A moment ago, the tone of his voice was totally different while admitting he'd been lucky to survive, and now he acted as if what had happened to him was just another day at the office.

When she'd seen the workout area in his home she could tell the equipment was state-of-the-art. Dean had hinted that Bobby still had a long way to go with his recovery. Hell, the man wasn't even allowed to drive.

"Honey, I think I need to go to the ladies' room." Racy latched on to her husband's arm as she inched her way out of the booth. "You want to come with me, Leeann?"

"Gladly."

"And since you all interrupted our girls-only party—" Racy poked a finger at her husband's chest "—you get to buy the next round."

"Hey, it wasn't my idea," Gage protested.

"It was mine," Bobby said, pausing in the midst of signing his autograph for one of the waitresses on her order pad. "I saw your table of pretty faces and just couldn't resist."

The waitress giggled as Bobby offered her a quick wink.

Leeann rolled her eyes. "Let's go, Racy."

They crossed the bar and entered the crowded ladies' room with only one open stall available.

"Do you mind?" Racy inched toward the door. "My ability to wait has dropped considerably."

"Go ahead. I'm just here to keep you company."

Racy grinned and closed the stall door. One by one the other ladies left the bathroom until Leeann and Racy remained, but the only sound was the running water as they stood side by side washing their hands.

"Go ahead, girlfriend." Leeann caught her friend's reflection in the mirror. "I know you've got something to say."

"I've got a lot to say, but we can't lock ourselves in here all night."

"And Maggie would never forgive us for excluding her." Leeann yanked a paper towel and dried her hands. "We've probably got seconds before someone walks in on us, so make it quick."

"Are you okay?"

Leeann sighed and tossed the towel in the trash. "I did say quick, right? Not sure I can answer that in thirty seconds or less."

"Look, I listened to all your ramblings before Bobby showed up tonight." Racy dried her hands, then gently laid one on Leeann's arm. "And I've just watched you being—well, being with him again for the first time in fourteen years."

"I'm not with him. Not like that."

"Okay, hanging around him. Is that better?"

Leeann nodded, wondering why she was making such a fuss over her friend's words.

"And while it's easy to say it's all so familiar, seeing the two of you together…it's not anywhere near the same, is it?"

"Stop trying so hard to be polite about all this craziness," Leeann replied with a smile. "You're not making much sense, but I get what you're saying."

"And what am I saying?"

"That I'm a withering mass of confusion and uncertainty. But it's fine." Leeann yanked the door open and waved her friend out. "There's always another margarita waiting out there with my name on it."

"Well, I don't think I said that exactly. If you ever want to talk, I'm here—" Racy cut her words short when they found Jackie, one of the assistant managers, waiting in the hall. "Hey, are you looking for me?"

"Your hubby said I could find you here. Can I drag you to the kitchen for a minicrisis?"

Racy headed off with her employee and Leeann walked back to the bar's main area. She paused when she saw that her friends still weren't back at the table and even Gage had disappeared. That left the racing champion holding court with about a half-dozen people. Striding up to them, she reached for the freshly poured margarita.

"No, I'm far from retirement," Bobby boasted, hoisting an icy beer in salute. "I've still got my eye on a few more prizes, including the all-around championship again."

"That new upstart driver you got on your team, Doug LeDoux, he's just a kid," a man standing nearby said. "But he's pulled off a few impressive finishes."

"That kid is twenty-three," Bobby replied with a grin. "Which, come to think of it, isn't too far from when I started. But yeah, he's fitting into the program real well."

"But your injuries?" one of the other fans asked. "They sounded really bad on the news—"

"Nothing to worry about," Bobby cut the second man off, the smile on his face slipping just a bit. "I'll be back behind the wheel in no time at all."

Leeann turned to look out at the dance floor, watching Justin and Gina as they showed Dean the fine art of line dancing. She was silently bewildered by every word coming from Bobby's mouth.

He wasn't fine. He could barely keep himself upright when she'd first seen him yesterday and earlier today he'd had a death grip on his cane.

Knock it off! The command was unvoiced, but just as powerful. *None of this is any of your business!*

Everyone around him seemed very happy with his assurances and soon drifted away. That left the two of them standing at the booth and Leeann realized she'd missed the opportunity to walk away while he'd been preoccupied with his adoring public.

"Well, I guess we're stuck here holding on to

the table, just like old times—unless you're planning on leaving again."

Was that a dig?

She tried to read the expression on his face, but the bar's low lighting and the Stetson he wore made it difficult. Then he backed up a step, almost stumbled and sank to the cushioned seat on one side of the booth, his hand gripping the table.

"Should I—do you want me to get Dean?"

He jerked his head up and looked at her. "What the hell for?"

Sighing, she sat across from him and placed her drink on the table. Conscious of the loud country music and that they were probably the subject of many curious stares, she leaned forward, waiting for him to follow her lead.

When he did, he also bumped up the brim of his Stetson and offered one of his famous Winslow smiles, but she could see the deep lines etched around his mouth and the firm set of his clenched jaw.

"Why are you lying to those people?" Leeann asked.

Bobby's smile stayed in place, but his fingers tightened around his beer bottle. "I don't know what you're talking about."

"Come on, Bobby, you're a walking wall of pain. Where is that cane you used earlier today? Should you even be on your feet right now?"

"I'm not on my feet."

She blew out a frustrated breath. "You know what I mean. I saw your exercise room today, remember? Besides the all-in-one home gym and a complete set of free weights, there's also a fancy therapy table, parallel bars and a piece of equipment Dean called a Hydrocollator Heating Unit. Not your typical workout equipment."

He took a long draw from his beer. "So? Like everything else in my place, I wanted it to be impressive."

Leeann ignored the way he threw the word she'd used to describe his house back at her and forged ahead. "Dean told me you should've stayed in that rehab center for another month."

His smile disappeared as he set his drink down. "Zip talks too much."

"He also said the only reason you were released was because you agreed to follow a strict program that I'm sure doesn't include a lot of walking, never mind alcohol or making promises you can't keep—like going back on the racing circuit."

"Zip is my physical therapist and my best friend." Bobby cut her off, his voice a hard whisper. "He's not my keeper and he won't be the one who decides when I get back behind the wheel of my race car. And neither will you."

Leeann ignored the way her heart clenched at those last words. But if he was going to peg her as a nosy busybody, she might as well go for the whole shebang. "You can't even drive a regular car yet because of the damage to your legs and spine. What makes you think you will ever race professionally again?"

"What makes you think it's any of your business?"

His harsh tone and the irritation that darkened his blue eyes to near black told her she'd gone too far. Again.

"It's not. You're right." She lifted her glass and took a long sip. "Do whatever you want. See if I care."

"I don't need to 'see' anything." He leaned even closer to her. "I know you don't care. All you ever cared about was modeling. Which has me wondering why you ever quit? So come on, Leeann, since you can't keep your nose out of my business, tell me why you walked away from the world of high fashion?"

Chapter Six

Leeann flinched, the sting of his words evident on her face.

But he didn't stop pushing, since she had no issue shoving him. "What? No answer? At least tell me where all this is coming from. We haven't seen or spoken to each other in years. I'm home for one day and now you're trying to psychoanalyze me?"

"No, but—"

"But what? You're pulling out some psychological mumbo jumbo you learned at the police academy?" he continued, unable to stop the words from rolling off his tongue. "Maybe you need to take a look at yourself, considering you've walked away from yet another job today."

"How did—who told you?"

"Gage mentioned that tonight's ladies-only party was your farewell from the sheriff's department and how sorry he was to see you go. Boy, you're throwing away careers left and right. A few years in New York, a few years back here. Where to next?"

She put her drink down hard, the glass almost tipping over before she caught it and set it upright. "Well, as much fun as this has been, I think it's best if I leave now." Leeann slid out of the booth. "Tell everyone I said good-night."

Stupid! Stupid! Stupid!

Bobby had dragged Zip to the Blue Creek Saloon tonight to try to get Leeann out of his head, especially after seeing her earlier today at the Youth Center.

Yeah, he'd stopped by on purpose during a

trip into town to show Zip downtown Destiny. The hero worshipping from the kids had been nice, but when Leeann had stepped out of an office to see what all the commotion was about, arms crossed and a fire in her eyes, he'd finished writing out a check to cover a group ski trip and hightailed it out of there.

Running into his old friend Justin Dillon when he'd arrived here had been great. Gage Steele had been standing there, too, and he'd made introductions for Zip, both of them meeting the other Cartwright brother, Landon. Then they'd heard the squealing and clapping from a distant table as Landon shared his impending fatherhood news.

He'd found his stare focused on the ladies, and even when Leeann spotted him, he hadn't turned away. After that, it didn't take long to convince the men to cross the bar. It felt like old times, standing directly behind where Leeann sat in the booth, back when they'd been young and in love—

Leeann rose and Bobby forced himself to his feet. Ignoring the burst of pain that started at his hip and raced southward to his knee, Bobby forced himself to his feet, cutting off her exit. "Wait, Lee, please. Don't go."

She stilled, but didn't look at him. She also didn't back away. A small victory. He'd take it.

"I'm sorry," he continued, "after all these years you'd think we could find something better to say to each other…"

Yanking off his Stetson, he dragged his fingers through his hair before slapping it back on his head. "Damned if I know what it is about you that still ignites a fire in my blood."

Her gaze flew to his, but she remained silent.

"Look, I appreciate your concern, I really do, but I can prove to you I'm fine."

"You don't have to prove anything to me, Bobby. You're right. We're just old…friends who haven't seen or spoken to each other in over a decade and suddenly we're taking stabs at each other. It doesn't make any sense."

He grinned. "When did our…friendship ever make sense? Besides, this won't include any talking."

Curiosity crossed her features. "You're not planning to do something stupid, are you?"

He hoped not. "Dance with me."

"What?" Her eyes grew wide. "Are you crazy?"

Probably, but he didn't care. His fingers still hummed from her brief touch earlier, and despite recognizing this new habit of hers of maintaining a well-defined personal space, he found himself wanting to invade that space. Wanting to wrap her in his arms and feel the press of her soft curves against him.

If that meant slogging through the shooting pain in his back and legs, so be it.

"We used to be pretty good at two-stepping if I remember correctly." He inched closer. "Unless you don't think you can keep up with me?"

An emotion flashed through her eyes so fast

he wasn't sure he'd actually seen it, much less be able to describe it.

"Lee? What's wrong?"

She blinked and it was gone. Squaring her shoulders, her chin jutted out in that familiar stubborn way. "Nothing. Let's do it."

At first he wasn't sure he'd heard her right, but when she headed for the dance floor, Bobby fell into step beside her, thankful his legs obeyed his silent command to move.

He placed his hand at her lower back, his fingertips brushing the soft cotton material of her T-shirt as they made their way through the crowd.

She flinched at his touch, but then they were at the edge of the well-worn parquet floor as a rocking hillbilly tune gave way to a classic George Strait ballad. She spun to face him. This time he was certain he saw a flare of panic in her eyes.

At what? Being in his arms again?

She started to shake her head. Before she could

put her protest into words, he snaked one hand around her waist, clasped her hand in his and made his way among the growing number of couples on the dance floor. She let him lead, but barely. Her free hand only just touched his shoulder, her arms unyielding, back rigid.

He looked down. Her gaze was locked on the open collar of his shirt, her bottom lip clenched between her teeth.

"Hey, if you're worried about people gossiping, no one's watching," he whispered into her hair above her ear. "It's just you and me."

He rubbed his thumb along her waist, trying to get her to relax, but the act seemed to make her even more tense. Damn, she was strung tight, moving across the dance floor like a puppet with an unseen power pulling at her strings.

Maybe this wasn't such a good idea.

Thanks to too much time on his feet his legs were on the edge of collapse, and obviously dancing with him was the last place she wanted to be.

What a joke.

He opened his mouth to tell her they should end this, when someone jostled her from behind. She landed hard against his chest and he grabbed her hips with both hands, bringing their bodies flush from the waist to the knees. He willed his already weak legs to hold him upright as he tightened his grip and spun in a quick half step in order to keep them from landing in a heap on the ground.

A small cry escaped her lips, her hands fisting his shirt as she clutched his shoulders.

"It's okay, Lee. I've got you."

She mumbled something so low he had to dip his head closer.

"Please...don't..."

The soft plea went straight to his gut.

He instantly eased his hold, but then his boot heel caught on the edge of the dance floor. He strained to keep them upright as a white-hot flash of pain raced down both legs, knifing through bone, muscle and memory to steal his breath.

Clenching his jaw, he battled against the blinding pulsation. "Damn! Not now!" His words hissed between his teeth.

Lee's head jerked up and her grip tightened. "Bobby? What is it?"

He opened his mouth, but nothing came out. He willed his legs not to give out on him.

"What can I do?" Her hands, suddenly strong and sure, moved to his back as she shifted her hips, trying to take on his weight. "Here, lean on me."

"No." He gutted out the words. "I'm…okay."

"Like hell you are. You need my help!"

Yeah, he did and he hated himself for it. "Get… get us off the dance floor."

Her head wrenched back and forth, the short strands of her hair whipping across his throat and jaw. "I don't see a place to sit."

He gestured with his head toward an area next to the stage. "Over there. The wall."

It was empty but dark. He hoped there was nothing on the ground to trip them up. He wrapped one arm around Leeann's shoulders, and she held him around his waist, plastering herself to his side as they took several shaky steps together.

It seemed to take forever, but finally they were close enough for him to brace one arm straight against the rough wood paneling, taking some of the weight off his legs. It wasn't enough. He pivoted Lee around to face him, then released her to use both arms to support himself, effectively blocking her between his body and the wall.

Much better.

The pain lessened and he was able to pull in a deep fortifying breath, bringing with it Leeann's fresh, clean scent that held a hint of earthy spice. A scent that had teased his memory long after she'd walked out of his house earlier today, only to wrap around him again when he'd leaned over the booth, using the first excuse he could think of to get close to her.

He lowered his head, gently bumping her forehead with the brim of his hat. "Man, you smell good."

Her hands fell from his waist and she tried to back away but the wall was right there. Tilting her head, she looked up at him, but it was too dark to see her face.

Her breaths, quick and hot, scorched his skin and he flexed his fingers, pressing them hard into the wall.

"Do you want me get some help?" she whispered, the earlier panic returning to her voice. "I can go find Dean."

"Stay." His request sounded like a demand. He cleared his throat and tried for a lighter tone. "This way it looks like I dragged you off the dance floor for some private time. Or maybe you dragged me."

"Bobby—"

"Don't worry, Lee. I'm not thinking about anything at the moment except trying not to fall on my ass and make a complete fool of myself."

That was a lie, but she didn't have to know that.

"Do you feel better?"

He must, because his lower half was starting to respond to the intimacy of their position, tightening with need for the warm, sexy woman only inches away. "Yeah, I think so. Just don't ask me to move."

"W-we can't stay here all night."

As long as she stood here with him, no farther away than a deep breath to bring their bodies together, he was fine. He doubted Leeann felt the same way, even if she did seem a bit more relaxed now that they were off the dance floor.

Was that because he wasn't actually touching her?

"Sorry about my lack of finesse out there."

"You had to prove a point, huh?"

"I'm not talking about my injuries. Before… you acted—I don't know…uncomfortable while we were dancing. Don't tell me the single guys in this town haven't been keeping you busy on the dance floor."

"No guy, um, what I mean is I don't have a..." Her gaze centered on his chest again, her voice so low he barely heard her. "I don't date. It's been a while since I've been out...dancing or anything else."

Was that a good thing?

Bobby had been surprised he hadn't seen a wedding ring on her finger. He'd always figured Leeann left her modeling career in order to settle down, probably with a rich businessman who reminded her of her father. To find her living here in their hometown, no boyfriend, and as of today, no job...

Something wasn't adding up.

But none of that mattered right now.

What mattered was that she was right here in front of him.

He dragged one hand down the paneling, inches away from Leeann's sweet curves. He wanted so much to touch her, to press up against her, to make her look up at him again so he could cover her mouth with his.

"Lee—"

He shifted the hand still pressed to the wall to get better support. Big mistake. His knees buckled. Leeann grabbed him, and while the heat of her touch did wonders for his libido, it wasn't going to keep them from falling flat on their faces.

"Lee, let go." The last thing he wanted was to take her down with him.

Then the familiar strength of Zip's muscular arm slid across Bobby's shoulder blades. "Hey, buddy! What ya doing over here? Making time with the prettiest lady in the place?"

Leeann jerked her hands back.

Bobby silently mourned the loss.

He tried to smile through the pain, thankful his friend was making it appear that they were just two guys talking smack over a girl, instead of making Bobby look like a cripple who needed his human cane. "You know me, spending time making time."

"Yeah, well, I may just have to arm wrestle you for this one." Zip's free hand rose and took on a familiar pose they used often during his therapy sessions. Elbow bent and flat, open palm. A high five with staying power. Bobby let go of the wall to latch on to it. "She's something special."

"Wait, it's not like that," Leeann protested. "We're not—I mean, he's not—"

"It's okay, darling." Zip lowered his voice and offered her a wink. "I know what's going on."

"Oh, lay off the charm, will ya, Zip?" Bobby groaned. "I'm hurting like a sonovabitch and you're flirting?"

"Come on, Ace. Let's take this outside." Zip looked around and then back at Leeann. "What's the fastest way out of here?"

"Through the back entrance, just past the kitchen." Leeann eased away from the wall. "I'll show you."

"Perfect. I parked out back." Zip glanced at

Bobby. "You okay to walk or do I have pull the fireman on ya?"

There was no freaking way he'd be carted out of here on his buddy's oversize shoulders. "I can make it."

"No numbness in your lower legs?"

"Hell, no, I can feel everything." Bobby faced Leeann. The last thing he wanted was for her to witness any more of this fiasco. "Well, thanks for the dance and the interesting conversation. Why don't you head back to your friends?"

Leeann crossed her arms over her chest. "You'll never get past the kitchen staff, never mind the alarm at the back door, without me."

Zip let loose a subdued whistle. "Beautiful and smart. This one's a keeper."

Bobby pushed off from the wall and yanked his Stetson low over his brow. "Shut up and walk, Zip."

"Ladies first."

Leeann moved in front of them and they followed. From the back it looked like one friend helping out another who'd had a few too many beers. Except each step was like walking on hot coals. Something Bobby had actually done once at a party at the Playboy Mansion. Only this time every step was like a volcanic fire eating at the bottoms of his boot-clad feet.

They entered the back hall where the lighting was brighter, and Bobby fixed his gaze on Leeann. He liked how her hair shined in the overhead lights. The short dark lengths barely brushed against her shoulders. Her T-shirt clung to her tiny waist and emphasized the curve of her hips encased in the skinny jeans she wore.

Leeann had always had the most amazing backside. If anything it had gotten better with age.

Appreciation filled him and he kept his eyes glued to her butt, the sight of those swaying hips making him forget about the pain.

Sort of.

"Mmm, mmm, mmm…"

Bobby tightened his grip on his friend's hand. "Not one word, Zip."

"Okay, boss man, whatever you say."

Leeann stood in front of the double swinging doors that led to the kitchen and waved them past. When they reached the back entrance, she punched in a code and pushed open the heavy metal door.

"Jeez, I guess being a cop comes in handy when needing a security password, huh?" Zip asked as they stepped outside into the parking lot.

Bobby's gaze crashed with Leeann's, and he saw a quiet resignation there before she looked away.

"Which car is yours?" she asked.

"We came in the blue pickup over there." Zip nodded to the left, reaching into his pocket and tossing Leeann the keys. "I wanted to bring the bird, but Ace here axed that idea."

Leeann hit the button to unlock the doors. "Bird?"

"Forget it." Bobby shot Zip a warning look. "It's not important."

When they reached the truck, Bobby waited until Leeann opened the door, then he grabbed the truck's inside frame and held on. "I've got it from here."

"You sure, Ace?" Zip asked.

"Yeah." His gaze flew to Leeann, who stood nearby, then back to his buddy. "Get behind the wheel, okay?"

Zip smiled and gestured to Leeann for the keys, easily catching them before heading for the other side of the truck. "Night, Leeann," he called out. "And thanks, I couldn't have gotten Twinkle Toes out of there without your help."

She returned Zip's wave, but her eyes remained on Bobby. Was she waiting to see how he got into the truck?

Fine.

Flinging his Stetson inside the cab, Bobby grabbed on to the inside assist handle and hoisted himself, twisting onto the front seat. The move hurt like hell and left him looking like a fool with his feet still hanging outside the truck, but at least he was sitting down.

Lacing his fingers beneath his left knee, he grunted through the pain and lifted his leg, dragging his foot inside the cab to save the additional strain on his back.

Then a strong yet feminine grip repeated the movement, lifting his right leg, supporting the knee before setting his foot gently to the truck's floor.

Bobby froze.

He stared at her hands, resting just above his knee. The warmth of her touch seeped through his jeans. His fingers stretched out for hers, but she jerked her hands away, clenching them together at her waist.

"Ah, I'm sorry..." Leeann waved one hand toward the building. "You know, about the dance."

"I'm not."

Her gaze shot to his.

"I enjoyed holding you in my arms again," he said. "Sort of like coming home."

Her eyes widened, her mouth dropping open in surprise.

"Let's do it again," he ventured, having no idea why he was pushing this. Yes, he did. It had felt good, damn good, to be so close to Leeann again. "Soon?"

Her lips moved into an easy smile. "Bobby, you can't even stand on your own two feet."

"At the moment, but when I'm better?"

"We'll see."

Zip barked out a laugh he tried to cover with a cough.

Bobby landed a light elbow to his friend's bicep, but didn't look away from Leeann. "You know when my mom used to say that, the answer was usually no."

"But every once in a while the answer was yes."

She stepped away from the truck, closed the

door and offered a quick wave before turning back toward the rear entrance of the bar.

Zip started the engine and flipped on the headlights, but didn't put the truck into gear until they saw Leeann disappear inside the building. "Man, tell me you're not going to do something stupid."

Bobby turned to his friend. "Like what?"

"Like let her go all over again."

Almost a week after the Blue Creek Saloon incident, Leeann could still feel Bobby's rough, warm touch on her hands. She clenched and released her fingers a few times, shaking them loose as she ran, her feet eating up miles of blacktop.

"Don't be silly, it's just—"

She couldn't finish her sentence because she didn't understand why her palms still tingled, as if she'd just laid her hands on him a moment ago.

Impossible because she'd avoided him for the past six days.

She'd cleaned her two-bedroom cottage from top to bottom, visited with her Aunt Ursula to sort out the beauty parlor gossip from the truth when it came to her and Bobby, and took care of his mother's garden in record time at the crack of dawn two mornings in a row to avoid an accidental encounter.

Worst of all, she'd only gone to the Youth Center after checking to make sure he wasn't there. Bad, but a necessity. The staff had said Bobby and Dean had stopped by twice during the week to visit with the kids in the after-school program.

Maggie and Racy had finally wrangled her into going to Laramie yesterday afternoon for lunch and shopping, but only after they'd sworn off the topic of Bobby Winslow.

After she'd gone back inside the bar that night, they'd cornered her for an explanation. She'd quickly explained away the rumor that Bobby was drunk, replacing it with the truth of what had happened when they'd danced.

Or tried to dance.

Between her acting like a cardboard cutout and his bad back they were lucky they didn't end up sprawled in the middle of the dance floor. Then again, the only thing her friends concentrated on was that she'd agreed to dance with her old boyfriend in the first place.

And every morning she ran.

Come rain or shine, Leeann donned her exercise gear, tied on her sneakers and headed out for her daily five miles.

Never in the direction of her pond or Bobby's house.

Of course, if she really thought about it, Bobby hadn't tried to see her either.

Was he still embarrassed by what had happened?

So caught up in the emotional upheaval of being near him again, she'd spent the evening lecturing him one minute and fighting off old memories, both good and bad, the next.

When it came to dealing with being held in

a man's arms—his arms—for the first time in years, she'd been so consumed by panic she hadn't given any thought to his discomfort.

She'd been uncomfortable enough for the both of them. Or so she thought until he had her backed against the wall. He had been seconds away from kissing—

"Ah, miss? Excuse me?"

A male voice interrupted Leeann's thoughts. She downshifted into an easy jog, noticing for the first time the silver SUV and white van behind it, moving at a snail's pace along the road.

"We're a bit lost. Maybe you can help?" The passenger in the SUV, a man in his late sixties with a trimmed gray beard and startling blue eyes, leaned out the window. "Is this County Road 389?"

Leeann looked around, realizing she'd unknowingly taken the turn that led straight out to Bobby's place, which was less than a hundred yards away. "Ah, yes, it is."

The man smiled, triggering a memory. Did she know him? Her training kicked in. Palming her cell phone in her jacket pocket, she proceeded with caution, slowing to a walk but staying a safe distance from the vehicle. "I'm guessing you and the white van are together?"

"Yes. We're looking for the Winslow place. We stopped at the diner in town and asked for directions, but they were pretty protective of their hometown celebrity."

A sudden desire to shield Bobby filled her as well.

"My name is Vincent Jameson. We're in town to do a photo shoot with Bobby Winslow." The man pulled a leather billfold from his shirt pocket. "I'll show you my identification if you don't believe me."

She believed him, connecting his name with his face. He was a famed photographer she'd worked with once many years ago. He obviously didn't recognize her, but Leeann wasn't surprised. She'd only been one of many models he must've worked with over the years and her looks had changed dramatically since New York. "No, that won't be necessary."

A familiar blue pickup came over the hill in the opposite direction and slowed to a stop when it reached them. "Hey, Leeann!" Dean leaned out the driver's-side window. "Let me guess? You found the people I was sent to look for."

The vehicles pulled to the side of the road and quick introductions were made. Then Dean made a U-turn, pulled up alongside her and called through the open passenger-side window, "Come on, hop in."

"Oh, no, I'm just out for a jog. I think I'll get back to it."

"And miss the chance to see Ace playing the part of a fashion model? You could give him a pointer or two."

She swallowed hard. "You know about my former career?"

Dean grinned. "Are you kidding? I still got my copies of *Sports Illustrated,* Swimsuit Editions

2003 and 2004. I think my favorite was the all-American bikini."

Her face heated with a hot blush. "Well, that was a long time ago and I don't want to get in the way."

"Don't you want to see how he's doing?" Dean's voice turned serious. "Your town isn't exactly a thriving metropolis, yet still you two have managed to stay clear of one another."

"He's avoiding me?"

"As much as you're avoiding him."

Uncertainty filled her. She hadn't been back to a photo shoot of any type since that night six years ago. It had taken a long time before she could face the simple flash from a digital camera without flinching or resurrecting memories of a time she wanted to keep firmly in her past.

"How is he doing?" she finally asked.

Dean's grin returned. "Why don't you come see for yourself?"

Chapter Seven

"Okay, everyone, let's break for a few minutes." Lowering his camera, the photographer rose from his crouched position. "This just isn't working."

Leeann couldn't agree more.

Dressed in a black tuxedo, tie hanging loose around his neck and a starched white shirt halfway unbuttoned, a whisper of stubble on his jaw and a drink in one hand, Bobby looked like he was doing just fine.

More than fine.

At least on the outside.

On the inside, however, she suspected he was fed up. He slumped in the corner of his leather couch looking sexily disheveled and casually shameless. But even with a blonde in a skintight dress sporting a neckline that plunged practically to her waist draped over his lap, he looked bored.

Not exactly the image needed to match the rough cut of the commercial they'd viewed less than an hour ago.

Leeann had been impressed with the imagery and the story that meshed a nineteenth-century cowboy waiting for his lady to return with a modern man doing the same, and yes, Bobby looked amazing on the film, but something wasn't working.

Her professional experience told her it was the model.

Windy—her real name, the girl had excitedly declared—was beautiful, but too young. Even with the couture gown and the magic of hairstyling and makeup she still looked barely out of her teens. Not the kind of woman a suave, debonair man would be waiting for.

"Okay, time to back off," Leeann whispered to herself, moving away from the crowded scene laid out in Bobby's formal living room. "Your opinion doesn't mean a thing here."

"I'd like to hear it anyway."

She turned and found Bobby standing behind her.

Close behind her.

Backing up, she moved toward the section of his home he'd already declared off-limits. Thanks to her tour last week, she knew this area housed his office and the master bedroom.

Despite that, she took a few more steps past an imaginary do-not-cross line. He followed, of course, staying within her personal space. Her habitual instinct to put distance between them didn't arise. The closeness wasn't bothering her as much as she thought it should.

Or was it because it was Bobby?

Pulling in a deep breath, her head filled with the same sharp and woodsy masculine scent she remembered from being in his arms last week. She wasn't a fragrance kind of girl, but he did smell good. Must be those men's bath care products he was promoting.

"Look, I'm just an uninvited visitor—"

He took another step toward her, the toes of his polished dress cowboy boots bumping against her running shoes. "Didn't I tell you I was happy you were here?"

Yes, he had, not hiding his surprise when he'd walked out on his front porch and saw her climb down from the truck Dean had parked in the circular drive. But other than exchanging quick hellos, they hadn't had a chance to talk as the crew unloaded their vans and the photographer's assistant had sent Bobby off to change his clothes.

Leeann had stayed clear of the controlled chaos, but enjoyed watching his living room transformed into a photo shoot, as the lighting was set up with reflective softbox umbrellas, backdrop panels raised and furniture moved.

For a moment she'd felt jarring fear, her heart tapping out a rapid beat that she accepted as a reaction to the past, but then Dean had appeared at her side.

He'd kept her busy answering his questions, some serious and some humorous. The more time passed, the more she found herself flooded with good memories from her years spent in this industry, instead of that one last terrible one. She'd been damn good at her job and she was proud of all she'd accomplished. Her therapist had always tried to get her to concentrate on the good stuff instead of those few hours that ended it all for her.

For the first time she was able to do just that.

"Come on, Lee. I'd really like to know what you think." Bobby drew her attention back to his original question as he waved a hand toward the set. "This was once your world. Even I've done enough of these things to realize that something is just...off."

Being proud of her past was one thing, sticking her nose in where it didn't belong was another. Jeez, hadn't she done enough of that with Bobby since he'd shown up back in town?

"It's not my place."

"Does your friend have something she'd like to share with us?" Vincent Jameson joined them. "This whole shoot was a rush job ordered by an executive from the product company. My assistant didn't have time to do a thorough sketch out, so I'm willing to listen to anything."

Leeann shook her head, wishing she'd kept the ball cap she'd been wearing on, instead of leaving it in the truck. "No, I really don't—"

"Hey, I know you." The photographer cut her off. "Don't I? You look really familiar."

Her smile felt forced, but it was the best she could do. "I'm Leeann Harris. We worked together a few times when I was with Elite."

"Of course!" Vincent snapped his fingers. "I

remember now, the long hair. Almost to your waist, right?"

Hands grabbing her, struggling to get free. Trying to run, the biting sting of her flowing hair yanking her backward to the floor, spindly fingers twisted in its length, holding her captive—

"Lee?"

She jerked away from Bobby's touch and blinked hard, bringing his and the photographer's puzzled expressions into focus. "Y-yes, I'm sorry, that's me. I used to—yes, I did have long hair back then."

"Yeah, it was so long it took you a while to get all the Bora Bora sand out of it after we shot for the swimsuit issue one year. I can understand why you finally cut it short. You're retired now?" Vincent asked.

Leeann tried to take a fortifying breath, but Bobby's gaze was so intent as he studied her it made her even more nervous. "Yes, I left the business about s-six years ago."

"So what do you think about today? You've certainly done enough of these shoots during your career. And we've only got today to get the film in the can."

She looked to Bobby to intercede, but he remained silent. Of course he did. Wasn't he just asking her the same thing?

She glanced outside to gather her thoughts, not surprised to find the blonde outside on the deck, happily flirting with Dean. "Well, my first impression is that it's a casting issue."

"Meaning Windy?"

Leeann nodded, racking her brain for the right words to not upset anyone. "She's very pretty, but Mr. Winslow is a bit—well, the age difference between them is very apparent when they pose together."

Oh, boy, was that diplomatic enough?

Vincent nodded. "Hmm, you do have a point."

"Why not have Leeann do it?"

What?

Leeann opened her mouth to protest, but was too stunned by Bobby's statement to speak.

"We're the same age and she's experienced at this stuff," he continued, a wide grin on his face. "It'll be great."

Was he crazy? Absolutely not! There was no way she was getting in front of the camera again.

"No, I don't think so." The words came out rough, but she was grateful to have found her voice. "Besides, you already have a model here."

"Who's not working out," Bobby pushed. "There's a clause in the contract that states I have a say in all production aspects. Including casting."

"But she was used in the filming of the commercial, which is already completed," the production assistant added, joining their group. "To change models now, especially with one so different in coloring and shape..."

Meaning she was a size six instead of the size two chatting it up with Jersey boy out in the sunshine.

Perfectly happy with her hard-won, toned body, Leeann was glad for the excuse. "Exactly, but what I was going to say is in the film footage, the woman's never seen clearly, only as an obscure, dreamlike figure to the cowboy."

Bobby started to speak, but Leeann cut him off. "Perhaps the still photography should be done the same way. I mean, after all, isn't the point to sell Mr. Winslow's endorsement of the product? Wear this, be like me and the girl will come back to you?"

She didn't give a damn what clause was in his contract. No way was she going to let him use the spoiled-star-getting-his-way card to get her back in front of the camera.

Vincent's eyes sparkled. "I think you've got something, Leeann. Perhaps you should be working on this side of the camera."

"I'm sure your staff would've come up with the same idea eventually." Leeann smiled. "Just happy I could help."

"Okay, let's get everyone back on set."

The assistant called out the order and the crew went back to work.

Leeann turned to Bobby. "I think that includes you, too."

"Lee—"

"Don't go there." She lowered her voice. "What the hell ever made you think I'd agree to such a harebrained idea?"

"Harebrained?" He fought hard not to smile and failed. "Gee, I didn't think it was that far off base."

"You have no idea how far off base it was."

He moved in closer, so much so that Leeann had to look up at him. "Tell me."

"What?"

"Tell me why you're so upset with my idea of you being in the photo shoot?" Bobby's voice dropped to a whisper to match hers. "I certainly seem to have hit a hot spot of yours."

"Should I start with how wrong it is to even suggest replacing a paid professional with an outsider?"

"Yeah, an outsider who at one time was one of the most photographed—"

"That was a long time ago!"

He stared at her until someone behind him cleared his throat in an obvious attempt to get his attention.

Leeann stepped back. "They're waiting on you."

"Don't leave."

She looked away and shook her head, tucking her hair behind one ear. "I'd really like...I just need a moment alone, okay?"

"There's a bathroom right there." Bobby pointed to a closed door. "Or my study is right next door. Feel free to wander, just don't leave. I think I'll be practicing my apology skills again once all this craziness is over."

He walked away.

Stay or go? Leeann didn't know what she wanted to do.

She could hear the photographer calling out instructions, pleased with whatever Bobby was giving him, but there was no way she could stay and watch.

Entering the bathroom, she closed the door behind her and stood in front of the mirror. Her reflection blurred until she saw a woman with long hair. The memories brought on by the photographer's comments tried to crowd into her head, but several deep breaths kept them away.

The vibration of her cell phone pulled Leeann from her thoughts. Seeing her aunt's name on the display, she realized she'd missed their lunch date.

"Sorry, Aunt Ursula, I didn't mean to forget about you," she said in greeting. "But you won't believe where I am."

"Hmm, sounds intriguing, honey." Her aunt's lyrical voice carried over the airwaves. Ursula was Leeann's mother's free-spirited and younger sister.

She'd moved to Destiny from Haight-Ashbury in San Francisco in the late seventies to help her sister care for Leeann when she was born. Deciding to stick around, she'd opened her own hair salon, Ursula's Updos. Over the years, Leeann and her aunt had formed an unbreakable bond.

"Since I'm stuck here anyway waiting on Minnie's perm to take hold, go ahead and spill the details! Does this have something to do with Mr. Winslow?"

Leeann sighed. While her parents had hated her dating Bobby back in high school, her aunt had always thought the boy considered no good by most people was just misunderstood. "You know, you always did have a soft spot for him."

"I wasn't the only one. Have you finally run into him again?"

"I'm at his place right now." Leeann decided to jump right in. "Talking to you from his guest bathroom while he's in the middle of a product endorsement photo shoot."

"Well, I wasn't expecting to hear all that. Are you okay?" Ursula's voice turned serious. "I mean, is being back in that kind of environment doing a number on you?"

Plopping down on the closed toilet seat, Leeann told her everything, including the memories she was holding at bay by sheer will.

"Maybe you shouldn't hold them off, honey," her aunt said. "If you let them come to you, if you deal with them head-on, it could be the best way to finally let go of your past."

"I have let go of my past," Leeann protested. "I moved on and created a whole new life for myself."

"A life that put you in control as a deputy sheriff, but even that wasn't fulfilling you in the way you'd hoped. Now that life has changed, and with Bobby back in the picture—"

She jumped to her feet. "What picture? There is no picture!"

"Sweetie, you're talking to me from inside his bathroom."

Leeann hated when her aunt pointed out the obvious. "Okay, you have a point, but Bobby is not back in my life. I don't even know if he's back in town for good."

"From what I've heard his house is pretty impressive."

A snort escaped before Leeann could slap a hand over her mouth. "Yeah, that seems to be the word for it, impressive. As in impersonal. Sort of like a cross between an art museum and *Little House on the Prairie.*"

Her aunt laughed. "Sounds like it needs a woman's touch."

"Not this woman." Leeann knew exactly where her aunt was going. "I've already told you, Bobby and I are just...old friends. We're not even friends anymore. We're more like acquaintances. Two people who used to be a part of each other's lives a long time ago."

"Like I said, he was your first love."

Leeann looked at herself again in the mirror, but remained silent. There was nothing she could say to refute the obvious.

"He was your *only* love."

Her stomach clenched at the truth in her aunt's words.

Her life in New York had been all about work, a social calendar that was more about self-promotion than relaxation and a crazy schedule that left her with little personal time.

There had been only a couple of men since Bobby, but none that she ever gave her heart to, and certainly no one in the past six years.

"Okay, I need to go, Auntie. I'll talk to you later."

She felt like a jerk for running her aunt off the phone but talking about the past with everything else she was trying to deal with today wasn't helping.

Deciding it was time to get out of this house, Leeann yanked open the door, stepped into the hall and slammed right into a mountain.

"Oh!"

She grabbed hold of Dean's shirt. He steadied her with one hand, the only casualty being a cardboard tube that bounced against the slate flooring.

"Boy, you never know who'll come walking

around a corner here." Dean gave a deep chuckle as he released her. "One minute a real live mannequin wearing little more than a bunch of lace and string strides by and now you!"

"Hmm, why do I get the feeling you're enjoying having a fashion model around to gawk at?" Leeann grinned as Dean bent over and picked up the cylinder.

"We've got two fashion models in the house. At least according to Bobby's bright idea."

Leeann rolled her eyes. "He told you about that, huh?"

"Don't be hard on him. He's just a guy, after all."

"I'll keep that in mind."

Dean grinned and pointed the tube at the door to her right. "Hey, would you mind putting this in Bobby's study? They're breaking for lunch and he's having some back spasms. I need to give him a quick rubdown."

She took the tube from him. "Sure."

"Thanks, doll."

Dean gave her a wink and took off for what Leeann guessed was the exercise room downstairs. She stepped into the next room, noticing the decorators had continued their mountain lodge/Western theme in here as well.

A massive desk sat on the far side of the room in front of an oversize window with a couple of leather chairs nearby. Against one wall was a table holding a two-level miniature replica of Bobby's house, right down to the grass, flowers and rocks.

Wow, that was really neat.

The exterior model showed how well the log mansion and the new outer buildings fit into the surrounding mountains and flatlands. It was breathtaking seeing it this way and Leeann realized Bobby had every right to be proud of what he'd built here.

Hanging on the wall above the model was an aerial photograph of the house and surrounding land. Leeann could easily see her pond just to the south. She lightly traced her fingers over the bright patch of blue peeking through the trees and the cylinder in her hand tipped upside down.

The lid fell off and sheets of rolled paper fell out.

"Oh, shoot."

She bent and picked up the thin sheets, noticing they were architectural drawings. The label on the tube read "Murphy Mountain Log Homes," the company that built this place. Was Bobby looking to do even more building out here?

Unable to resist, she spread out the papers on his desk. She could tell it was the large parcel of land down past the outer storage buildings and barn.

Thickly forested, it had remained untouched by her family for the four generations they'd owned it, but when a second transparent drawing slid into place over it, a large oval shape blocked out many of the trees and even more buildings dotted the landscape.

What was that? *My goodness, it looks like a—*

"So, what do you think?"

The sounds of Bobby's voice had Leeann spinning around.

He leaned heavily against the doorjamb, wearing the same faded jeans he'd had on when she first arrived. The flannel shirt was back, too, but now it hung open—revealing a flat stomach—as if he'd just pulled it on.

"Ah, I'm sorry." She waved at the paperwork. "Dean just asked me to drop these off in here, but they fell out of the tube in the process. I should have just put them back, but I was curious. It's not my place, I shouldn't have looked at them."

"You're right." He entered the room. "But you did and if I know you, you've got something to say about them."

Leeann looked back at the drawings. "I'm not even completely sure what I'm looking at. Is that a racetrack?"

Bobby nodded. "Regulation size, complete with viewing bleachers and a test facility. I figured with all this land my next plan was to move my racing operation here to Destiny."

Shocked, she dragged the two drawings back and forth across each other. Each time the sight of all those trees and precious open spaces disappearing tore at her heart.

Guilt for selling the land filled her. A necessity in order to save her aunt's life, the money went to pay the exorbitant cancer treatment bills. But what if she hadn't? Would this area never have been at risk of being destroyed?

"Isn't there something else? Something better you can do with all that land?"

"Something better?" He took a step closer. "You know, I bailed on a back rub so I could find you to apologize for earlier—"

"Forget the apology. How can you destroy all that forest?"

"Because I paid for it?"

"And that means you get to do whatever you want with it?"

"It's *my* land. Unless you've got a better idea?"

He shoved his fingers through his hair and blew out a frustrated breath. "Jeez, what is with you, huh? You don't like it that I'm rich, you've already decided my racing career is over. I thought maybe we were finally getting— I swear, it's one step forward, two steps back with you, Lee."

"You want a better idea? Fine." Her mind raced as she fought to come up with something—*anything*—Bobby could do with all that acreage. "How about a summer camp?"

"A summer what?"

"The Shipman Summer Camp closed down about ten years ago when Ron Shipman died. His kids sold the land and it's now a housing subdivision."

"So?"

"So the kids in this area, and I don't mean just Destiny, but the whole county, don't have any place locally to go in the summertime." She brushed past him, stopping to stand in front of the framed image of the land. "You've been down to the Youth Center and seen how busy it is, and that's during the school year. Can you imagine what this town is like when school is out and the kids don't have anywhere to go?"

"Lee—"

She spun back around, the idea flourishing to life as she spoke. She could see the camp where she and her friends, including Bobby, had worked all those years ago. She could see another camp being a part of this town, being here for a new generation to enjoy.

Her smile faded when she saw the incredulity on his face. "Well, you did ask for an idea."

"That's some idea."

She knew that tone. He'd already nixed the plan before he'd even had a chance to think it over. "I guess a person would have to put more time, personal attention and money into a venture like that than they'd ever get back."

"It's not just the money—"

"Hey, Ace, there you are! I've only got a few minutes to work my magic before they're going to call you back." Dean poked his head into the room. His eyes widened. "Sorry, guys. I didn't mean to interrupt."

"That's all right." Leeann tossed the empty cylinder onto the desk. "I think I'm finished here anyway."

Chapter Eight

Was he out of his mind?

Leaning heavily on his cane, Bobby stood in the conference room of Murphy Mountain Log Homes, a sprawling timber frame building, and thought back on the call he'd made less than thirty-six hours ago.

Nolan Murphy, the second eldest of the Murphy brothers and lead architect of the family business, had agreed to revise the already completed designs for Bobby's land.

Actually, what Bobby had asked for was a new set of plans.

All because he couldn't forget the disappointment he'd seen in Leeann's eyes when she'd stood in his office last Saturday.

Dammit, that wasn't entirely true either.

What he couldn't get out of his head was the way her eyes had lit up with enthusiasm when she'd tossed out her idea of what to do with his land. For a few moments, her joy had erased that haunted look that always seemed to linger in her eyes.

He wanted to erase that look forever and if that meant giving up his plans for a racing facility here in Destiny, fine. He already had one in North Carolina anyway.

But a summer camp for kids?

Yes, he had great memories of his summers at Shipman, both as a camper, thanks to a scholarship program for those unable to afford the fees, and as a camp counselor while in high school.

But did he have the desire to re-create the experience?

"No, it's something—oh, hell, someone else—

you desire," he muttered, shaking his head as he moved to sit at the table dominating the room, sinking into the plush seating.

Which is why he'd made the call to Nolan late Monday night.

During a brief discussion, they batted around some ideas and agreed to touch base the next day. Zip had been working him hard this morning when Nolan called back midsession asking if Bobby was available to meet. He'd agreed and cut the therapy short, hence the cane.

Gently massaging his left leg, Bobby was proud of the fact he'd been pain free the last week, even if he felt a bit wobbly today. Thanks to home-cooked meals instead of hospital food and Zip's workouts, he was gaining weight again and most of that was muscle. He felt strong and confident, two things that had sorely been lacking in his life ever since the accident.

Neither of which explained why he was even entertaining this crazy idea. "The things a guy will do for a woman."

"Did you say something?" Nolan Murphy entered the room, a set of drawings in his hand. "I didn't quite catch that."

"Ah, no, it's nothing." Bobby sat up straight. "Just talking to myself."

"Yeah, I do that a lot, too. With three teenagers at home I'm the only one who listens to me." Nolan sat opposite him, laying a cell phone on the table. "Sorry for the delay. I had to take a long-distance call from my brother."

Bobby wondered which one as there were six Murphy brothers, only four of whom were part of the family business. He'd gotten to know them quite well in the past year of working with the company.

"I ran into Liam when I first got here and then Dev and I reviewed an update to my security software," he said. "Don't tell me it was Bryant on the phone? Dev said he's not due back from his honeymoon for another week."

Nolan shook his head. "No, it was my oldest brother, Adam, calling from Afghanistan."

Ah, the one brother he hadn't met.

Bobby didn't really know Adam as he was at least six years older than he and the rest of their high school crowd. Like his brothers, Adam was an owner in the company, although he didn't work there full-time. "You've said he's in the Air Force, right?"

"Yeah, the reserves, but he might as well be active duty as much as he's been gone. He's due to retire early next year. His unit is on their third tour in the last five years."

"Has he been stateside recently?"

"This past summer." Nolan's tone grew serious. "He got a week's leave when he escorted the body of his best friend home, a member of his unit who was killed over there."

"Scott Coggen," Bobby said, picturing the framed photo draped with a gold star banner on the memorial wall at the Blue Creek Saloon.

Nolan nodded. "That was a tough week for Adam. He and Scott had been tight since high school. Still, with the services and…everything else I think he was almost glad to head back overseas this time."

Silence filled the room for a moment before Nolan flattened a hand over the drawings before him. "Okay, enough about that. Let's talk about this idea of yours." He smiled and raised his brows. "I'll have you know I only picked up your after-hours call because you've already dropped a bundle of money with my company."

Bobby returned Nolan's grin. "So you told me on the phone. Weren't you also waiting for your daughter to get home from a date?"

"Don't remind me," Nolan groaned and turned the papers around so they were faceup to Bobby. "Now, this is just a preliminary, off-the-shelf rendering for fifteen or so buildings that could be used for a summer camp. It's quite a departure from what you wanted earlier."

"Yeah, I guess it is."

Bobby didn't want to go into the reasons for the change, since he wasn't quite sure himself.

Leaning forward, Bobby kept his gaze on the

drawings as Nolan laid out the plans, sharing that they'd originally been drawn up for a millionaire who wanted to create a summer retreat for his family but eventually scuttled the idea.

The layout included a main building that could be used for offices and a medical facility while another structure would house a cafeteria. The smaller units, with modifications, would be the sleeping quarters for campers and staff.

"You plan on keeping the home itself private?" Nolan asked.

Bobby looked across the table at the architect, a bit dazed from all the information. "Ah, yeah. Private."

"I figured as much, but just so you know these plans don't include the barn or any of the other buildings we've already built for you until you want them included." He pointed at the cluster of squares in the clearing. "Of course, you'd need outdoor amenities like a ball field, campfire areas and so on. As is stands, this layout would accommodate approximately a hundred and twenty kids."

A hundred and twenty? What the hell was Bobby thinking?

"Of course, that depends on how many camp sessions you have. Also, I'd recommend you keep the access road outlined in the original plan." Nolan noted the property line off the country road. "It's far enough past your private drive that it could be the main entrance for Winslow Acres."

"Winslow what?"

"Sorry, just a name I came up with while playing around with the idea." Nolan grinned. "Naming the camp is the least of your worries. Are you going to run the place or are you just the money behind it?"

Run it? "Well, my rehab is right on schedule to get me back behind the wheel. The racing season runs from March through October. I won't even be in Destiny over the summer months, if all goes according to plan."

Confusion colored Nolan's features as his gaze flickered to the cane for a moment. "I was under the impression you might be retiring and moving back home for good."

The assumption burned, no matter how well-founded. "I'm not retiring. Like I told you on the phone, this is just a…a last-minute, off-the-cuff idea for what to do with the land."

"Which is why you requested I handle this personally instead of passing it to someone else on my staff?" Nolan sat back in his chair. "No sense in word leaking out and getting the town worked up over this, especially if it's just a pipe dream."

"Exactly."

A pipe dream. A fabrication. A spontaneous response to a woman who once meant everything to him.

Bobby stared at the drawings and then at the man whose company had worked hard to make Bobby's dream home a reality. Was he going to ask the Murphys to do it again?

For Leeann this time?

Nolan held his gaze for a long moment before he spoke. "Well, like I said, this is all very basic. Most owners who have the opportunity to build from the ground up would probably want to customize the plans so everything, from the location of the cabins to water access, is how they imagine the camp being once it's completed."

"Water access?"

"You know, for swimming, boating, et cetera?"

Jeez, the only thing swimming at the moment was his head. He hadn't thought there was much more to a camp than a few cabins. "Well, you've certainly covered all the bases in such a short amount of time."

"With six brothers, all within a few years of each other, my folks never sent us to summer camp. But my kids went many summers when we lived in Boston. Believe me, deciding on one is like picking out a college." Nolan stood and rolled up the drawings before dropping them into the carrying tube. "And speaking of water,

I know the pond next to your place isn't part of your property, but if this idea ever moves from 'what if' to something real, you might want to think about getting your hands on it."

Leeann's pond.

Yeah, he wanted to get his hands on—

The cell phone on the table vibrated. Nolan grabbed it and turned it over. "Ah, joy. The ex-wife."

Bobby pushed himself to his feet. "I'll let you get that."

"No rush." Nolan pocketed the phone. "It's a text message and I hate responding to those. Carrie knows that, which is why she sends them. She can wait."

Walking around the table, Bobby took the tube Nolan offered and then shook his hand. "I appreciate you pulling this together so quickly for me."

"I know there's more to this than you're telling me, but hey, every man is allowed his secrets. And these plans can stay hidden in that tube until you make up your mind about what you want to do," Nolan said as they walked out to the main entrance. "But we're into October now so if you choose to do any land clearing before winter sets in, no matter which plans we go with, we'll need to get moving soon. Especially if you keep on course with the racetrack."

Meaning clearing land for a racetrack was a lot different than clearing selected areas for a summer camp where the forest would be as much a part of the surroundings as the buildings.

Leeann's horror at cutting down all those trees flashed through his mind, but he forced the image back. It was his land, not hers. Not anymore.

"Understood," Bobby said.

They walked into the large entry area that acted as a lobby and found Zip leaning against the reception desk, chatting with the pretty red-head sitting there.

"You know, your friend has been talking to my receptionist since you arrived," Nolan said.

"Don't worry, Zip's harmless." Bobby noticed the sparkle in the girl's eyes and how it faded when she spotted her boss. "Most of the time."

Moments later, Bobby and Zip said their good-byes and climbed into the pickup truck.

"You want to share what that's all about?" Zip asked, nodding toward the tube lying on the seat between them as he pulled out of the parking lot. "I thought you got your phase two plans last week."

"I did, but…"

"But what? Your ex-girlfriend got a peek at your designs and didn't approve, so you're changing…" Zip's voice faded when Bobby remained silent.

"Really, Ace?"

Bobby should've known his friend would figure out what was going on, even after he'd refused to talk about the scene Zip had walked in on in his office.

"Just drive and I'll explain everything."

"You can explain when we get back to your

therapy session. We don't want to lose any ground on you regaining your full strength, right?"

His buddy was right, but the need to see Leeann, to show her the plans, burned deep inside him. Dazed from everything Nolan had said, from buildings to staff to water sports, he wanted to talk about all of it with the woman who'd stuck this crazy idea in his head.

"Don't you have a conference call with your business manager after lunch?" Zip continued, breaking into his thoughts. "And you mentioned checking in with your mom since her trip has her in someplace like Slovakia or Bratislava?"

"Bratislava is the capital of Slovakia, and what are you? My personal secretary?" Bobby looked at his friend. "How do you remember all this stuff?"

"Hey, except not knowing the capital of some middle European country, I'm a pretty smart guy. There's more to me than just muscles and a pretty face."

Bobby laughed and shook his head. "Okay, Zip, you win. It's back to the house. For now."

"And where will we be going this afternoon? I've got plans with that cute redhead tonight."

"Didn't you spend last weekend with that model?"

"Yeah, Windy and I enjoyed some of Cheyenne's nightlife before she flew out on Sunday." Zip shrugged. "You know, you also used to have a pretty active social life, BTA."

BTA. Zip's shortcut for "before the accident." His friend was right. There was a time when Bobby divided his time between bevies of beautiful women, from fashion models to advertising executives.

Funny how he didn't miss any of them.

In fact, holding Leeann in his arms that night in the bar was the first time in a long time that his body responded with basic male need. It was a moment that made him realize how much he wanted the connection again.

With no one but Leeann.

"You know, it might be time for you to get back out there." Zip offered him a wink. "So I'll ask again, where do you think you might find her this afternoon?"

"We'll start at the Youth Center." Bobby didn't bother to even question the "her" his friend was referring to. If Leeann wasn't there, he'd make a few phones calls, first to the Circle S Ranch and the Blue Creek Saloon. "If she's not there, I'll call in some backup if I have to."

"The point of always going out in a group is having backup in case you need it," Leeann said to the half-dozen high school girls gathered in front of her, all dressed alike in workout gear and sneakers. "Safety in numbers, right?"

The girls nodded. They were in their second of four self-defense courses Leeann taught at the Youth Center. The room she used wasn't large, which is why she kept the class limited to eight girls, but it was private.

"Last week we talked about how the first and

best weapon you have is your mind. Thinking about your surroundings and the people in it and listening to your gut instincts will keep you out of trouble most of the time." Leeann moved into the center of an oversize cushioned floor mat. "But there may be an instant when you find yourself alone and in a situation where you need to take action. So now we're going to put those blocking and releasing moves we talked about into practice."

She paired the girls up and, between the giggles and wisecracks, she got them practicing on each other. As she walked among them, she corrected positions, demonstrated techniques and enjoyed seeing the accomplishment in their eyes when they completed a maneuver.

Glancing at the clock, she noted the hour was almost up and Ben was running late. A member of the sheriff's department, Ben Dwyer often stopped by and acted as her tackling dummy, allowing her to show off moves—female versus male—against him.

Something that always impressed the girls as his entrance came unannounced.

He'd walk in, dressed in street clothes, and move in behind her. Never quite sure what she needed to do in order to get free, Leeann found she liked the surprise as it kept her own training sharp.

The door at the back of the room opened. Looking into the reflection on the mirrored wall, she froze when Bobby entered the room. Right behind him was Ben, who didn't pause but headed right toward her.

Realizing she wasn't in an open area, she quickly moved away from the girls just as her former coworker reached out and grabbed her by her arm. Spinning around, she braced for his response, but realized that not only had the girls noticed what was going on, Bobby had, too.

He raced across the room, rage in his eyes, his focus entirely on her make-believe attacker. Breaking Ben's hold, she twisted and flipped him over her shoulder. The girls cried out and backed away as poor Ben landed facedown on the mat, her foot on his back as a symbol of his submission.

And it kept Leeann between him and Bobby.

"It's okay." She turned and held out her hand, stopping his forward movement just as he reached her. "I'm okay."

Her palm landed on his chest and even with a heavy leather jacket on, she could feel his heart pounding, his gaze focused on Ben.

Leeann released her hold on her hapless victim in order to face Bobby completely, reaching up to cradle his jaw in her hands. She gently forced him to look at her; his skin was smooth beneath her touch, as if he'd just shaved.

Which was crazy because it was four in the afternoon.

"Bobby, look at me. I'm fine." She kept her voice low but firm as she kept talking. "He didn't hurt me. He wasn't going to hurt me, but if he planned to I can handle it. I did handle it."

She saw the moment she got through to him.

His eyes softened as he looked down at her, then he blinked and backed up a step, taking her with him because she hadn't let go.

"You're okay?"

His lips moved, but his words were barely a whisper, more like a silent plea.

She nodded. He reached for her before he clenched his hands in tight fists, dropped them to his side and took another step back, breaking free of her touch.

Ignoring the regret that filled her, Leeann turned back and helped Ben—who was still trying to catch the wind she'd knocked out of him—to his feet. She then made introductions to everyone, assuring them the intrusion was staged.

"You, too, Mr. Winslow?" one of girls asked. "You were supposed to come in and see Leeann get attacked?"

Leeann blinked hard at the girl's words, her gaze going straight to Bobby's reflection in the mirror.

"Um, no…" His voice trailed off for a moment when he caught her watching him. His embarrassment seemed to grow, then shift into another emotion completely. Confusion? No, that couldn't be right.

"I stopped by to…discuss something with her." Bobby broke free and graced the teen with his trademark smile. "With Leeann. I'm sorry. I shouldn't have interrupted your class."

"It's a good thing Leeann saw you coming to her rescue." Ben grinned as he rubbed a shoulder. "Otherwise, I'd be toast."

"Yeah, sorry about that," Bobby said.

"What do you have to be sorry about? She's the one who planted me on my face."

"Well, I'm sorry for disrupting things." He looked at her for a moment, backing away from the group. "I'll see myself out."

Once across the room, Bobby easily bent over to pick up whatever it was he had dropped—his cane? He then disappeared out the door.

"Ben, would you mind working with the girls

for a few minutes?" Leeann asked. "I really need to—you know—"

"Sure, I can stick around. As long as you haven't taught any of them that shoulder-flip move yet."

The girls laughed and paired off again. Leeann knew she was leaving them in capable hands as she hurried out of the room. Her eyes scanned the open area, spotting a volunteer and a student teacher from the elementary school. Leeann gestured to the door behind her and the teacher pointed toward the office.

She took off at a run and reached the lobby just as Bobby passed the volunteer's break room, heading for the front doors. "Hey!"

He stopped and turned, his cane and a familiar-looking cardboard tube in one hand. "Hey, yourself."

Stopping in front of him, Leeann tried to catch her breath, but the intensity in his stare made it more difficult than it should have. "So what was all that back there?"

"If you need me to explain it you…"

She shook her head. "No, what I mean is, why are you here? And why aren't you using your cane?"

"I'm not using my cane because evidently I don't need it." Bobby thrust the tube into her hands. "And here, this is for you."

"Me?"

"Look them over and tell me what you think. It was your bright idea after all."

"My idea?" She didn't have any clue what he was talking about. "Wait a minute, is this because of what I said in your office about your land?"

Bobby moved in closer and gently laid a finger at her lips, cutting off her words.

"This is going forward on two conditions. First, no one in town finds out about it until a final decision is made. Right now this is nothing but a crazy idea. And two, you're going to be part of it, from start to finish."

A delighted shock radiated through Leeann's

body. He'd done it? He'd really talked to one of the Murphys about her idea?

They hadn't seen or spoken to each other since the photo shoot five days ago. After the way she'd walked out of his office, she figured she'd be hearing the sound of bulldozers the next time she stopped by her pond.

Just as quickly her shock turned to panic and she shook off his touch. "I don't know the first thing about architectural drawings or building a summer—" Leeann cut off her words. She continued in a hushed tone, "I don't have the skills or experience for something like this."

"Perfect, we'll fumble through it together." Bobby grabbed a marker off a nearby table and scribbled a number on the outside of the tube. "Call me if you're up for the challenge. Otherwise the whole deal is off."

Chapter Nine

After almost a week of meetings where what needed to be done to turn twenty acres of natural forest into a summer camp for kids was discussed at length, Leeann had learned a few things.

Like there were summer camps that actually specialized in forensics, circus life or robotics. That Bobby was a pretty good cook and an even better patient, Leeann having witnessed first-hand a few of his sessions with Dean. And lastly, no matter how hard she tried, Daisy was never going to like her.

Leeann had done everything she could think of to get in the pup's good graces. Chew toys in all shapes and sizes, gourmet doggie treats and even sneaking the rascal some of Bobby's amazing lasagna after dinner one night.

Nothing.

"You should be happy she tolerates your presence," Leeann muttered to herself as she sat on her bed to tug on her sneakers. "And she finally stopped growling every time Bobby touches you."

Something he did a lot.

Something she was surprised to find she wasn't minding.

It had started when she'd shown up at his house the same afternoon he'd given her the plans for the camp and agreed to his terms. An agreement he'd sealed with a prolonged handshake she couldn't figure a polite way to refuse.

His hand, big and warm, felt familiar as it engulfed hers, causing those same tingles she'd experienced when he'd pulled her into his arms that night at the bar.

Only this time there hadn't been any fear or automatic pullback on her part.

A fact she'd only realized after he'd kept ahold of her, drawing her into his dining room, insisting the room was the perfect spot for them to work on their project.

She'd been at his place every day since, sometimes for hours, using the hand-peeled, aspen log dining table as the command center. It came complete with two laptops, the plans and—thanks to Dean who'd invaded a bookstore during a trip to Cheyenne—books that covered a variety of topics from child psychology to rustic interior design.

Their hands often collided as they stayed and rearranged tiny blocks from the three-dimensional model Bobby had borrowed to allow them to visually see how the camp might look once completed.

Or his arms would brush against hers when he'd lean over her shoulder and type into the computer a website for an already established camp. Then he'd stay close, pointing out whatever caught his eye, their faces inches from each other as they talked, debated and usually argued, often with Dean acting as tiebreaker or referee.

Bobby hadn't actually said for sure he planned to go ahead with the camp or talk about who would handle the day-to-day operations. Leeann found herself not wanting to push those issues yet.

She figured she'd done enough pushing when it came to the man's life the first couple of days. Besides, she was enjoying the time spent in Bobby's company.

"Admit it, girl, you are loving every minute of being with him," Leeann said to her reflection in the mirror over her dresser, finally admitting the truth aloud.

She loved being with Bobby again.

And repeating it made it more real?

Not willing to answer that question, she wandered into her living room and did the needed stretches before heading out for her daily run.

Leaving her small front yard, she noted the

time, almost ten o'clock. Bobby and Dean should be in Cheyenne by now for an appointment with a specialist to gauge Bobby's recovery.

He hadn't used the cane in the past week, at least not when she was around, and he only tired or was uncomfortable if they sat too long at the table. When that happened they'd moved their discussions to the family room, especially since meals were usually eaten at the counter in the kitchen.

His home still needed a personal touch—some plants, a crazy quilt or two like the ones her aunt pulled together from scraps of old fabric and maybe a few photographs that didn't include someone famous. But Leeann was finding she felt more and more at ease there.

Or was it because she was becoming more comfortable with Bobby?

When he traded jokes and wisecracks with Dean or she caught him staring at her, his eyes revealing a banked desire, she saw glimpses of the boy she'd known all those years ago.

She found herself torn over her growing feelings for the man he'd become away from the stardom.

Was that a good thing?

She hadn't been involved with anyone since New York, hadn't even wanted to. And of all people to be attracted to, was it wise to latch on to someone from the past? Especially when she had no idea what Bobby's future plans were.

For the camp or for himself.

Concentrating on the steady, rhythmic thuds of her feet hitting the pavement, Leeann worked to clear her head and reach the Zen-like state running always provided.

Enjoy the moment, enjoy today. Stick with your daily plan and everything else will fall into line.

Ten miles completed in less than ninety minutes and she was done, sweaty and tired, but it was a good tired. Slowing her pace as she entered her neighborhood, she noticed a shiny red sports car as she approached her house.

Bobby sat behind the wheel.

She slowed to a walk and found herself returning his familiar grin as he caught her staring. Hands on her hips, she crossed the last few feet to where the antique two-seater convertible sat parked against the curb.

"Well, look at you." Her words came out between heavy breaths that she quickly blamed on the running, not the gorgeous man smiling up at her. To emphasize that fact, she swiped the back of her hand across her sweaty forehead. "That's quite a car."

"A 1956 Ford Thunderbird." Pride laced his voice. "With a 312-cubic-inch V-8 engine, fully restored to the original factory specifications. The hardtop is back at the house."

"A Thunderbird—bird…" Leeann quickly put the connection together. "This is what Dean meant that night at the bar when he said he wanted to bring the bird."

"Yeah, like I'd ever let him get behind the wheel of this baby."

Leeann smiled. "Are you sure *you* should be behind the wheel?"

"Fully cleared to drive by the doc at this morning's appointment, as long as I take things slow and don't spend too much time driving at first." Bobby lovingly ran a hand over the steering wheel. "Of course, I grabbed the keys as soon as we got home."

She could see how much he loved the car, but even more importantly the freedom of being allowed to drive again. Did that mean being back in his race car wasn't far behind?

"It was just an idea. If you're busy or have other plans, I understand."

Leeann realized she'd missed what Bobby had said. "I'm sorry, what was that?"

"I asked if you wanted to come for a ride with me."

Oh, my, how long had it been since she and Bobby had been in a car together? "Really?"

"Yes, really. I want to talk to you about something, and I figured I'd use the open road as an incentive."

Hmm, now she was curious. "Well, I need to shower and change first. It won't take me long, thirty minutes tops."

"Go ahead." He waved at her house. "I'll wait."

The instinct to invite him inside her house had Leeann biting hard on her bottom lip. Should she? It was the polite thing to do, but he'd be the first man to cross the threshold since the day she'd moved in.

"Would you like to come inside?" The words tumbled from her mouth. She waited for the panic, but it never rose. "You can pull into the driveway behind my car if you want."

Bobby's grin widened. "Sure."

Walking across the yard, Leeann headed for her front door as Bobby parked. She got her key from the hidden pocket in her shorts, almost dropping it when she felt him move in behind her.

It took two tries to get the door unlocked. She

prayed he didn't notice. They stepped inside, directly into her living room. At just over a thousand square feet, her entire two-bedroom cottage could easily fit in Bobby's mansion many times over.

"This is *my* humble abode." Her mouth went dry as Bobby closed the door behind them. She needed water. Now. "I need—w-would you like something to drink?"

Bobby shook his head. He stayed in one spot, but his gaze moved around the room. "No, thanks."

"Why don't you have a seat?" She escaped into her kitchen and grabbed a water bottle from the refrigerator. Gulping the cold liquid even though she knew she shouldn't, she braced one hand against the sink and took a moment to steady herself.

It's just Bobby.

She repeated the words to herself as she returned to her living room to find that instead of sitting down, he'd moved farther into the space, looking up at the shelf that ran the length of all three walls.

"Wow, that's a lot of teapots." He turned to her. "How many do you have?"

"Over fifty, I think. I haven't counted them in a while."

"You been collecting them long?"

"I started back when I was modeling." She paused, but when Bobby just looked at her, she realized he was waiting for her to continue. "Some of the other girls were caffeine junkies, surviving on diet soda and coffee. I didn't like either, but thanks to my mother, I was always a big tea drinker."

He nodded. "I remember that about you."

Pushing another mouthful of water past the sudden lump in her throat, Leeann moved toward the short hallway, pointing to where the shelving began. "I found my first, the porcelain one with the fall leaves, in a little shop in Greenwich Village. I was feeling pretty homesick by then and the colors reminded me of Destiny in autumn…so I bought it. After that I picked them up whenever I was on location somewhere."

Thank goodness her aunt had the foresight to arrange for all of Leeann's belongings to be packed and shipped home after she'd rescued her. The boxes had sat in Ursula's garage until Leeann found the strength to go through everything, keeping what was important—like her teapots—but getting rid of most everything else. It had been therapeutic in a way, allowing her to pick and choose what memories of that time in her life she wanted to hold on to.

Leeann tried to see her place through his eyes, wondering what he thought. Did he see the warmth and coziness she'd tried to create with the simple furniture, her collection, even a quilt she'd made herself under Ursula's guidance?

"Is this from high school?" Bobby picked up a framed picture from a grouping on the end table near her couch.

"Yes, senior year." She couldn't see the image, but she knew which one it was by the frame.

Her favorite. It showed three best friends—her, Maggie and Racy—with their arms around each other's shoulders, grinning for the camera. She'd had that picture with her the entire time she'd lived in New York. "That was taken outside Sherry's Diner a few weeks before graduation."

"I know. I'm in the background."

"What?"

He turned the frame around and pointed to a corner of the photograph. "That's me. Watching you."

Leeann took the picture from his outstretched hand. She looked at it closely and saw he was right. Dressed in jeans and a T-shirt, a much younger Bobby leaned against the diner, his gaze on the three of them. How could she have missed that all these years?

"I—I never realized that." Her fingers slowly moved over the glass, tracing his image. "You were with me all that time."

Silence filled the air until Leeann looked up at Bobby. A powerful array of emotions filled his eyes, emotions she didn't want to—or couldn't—handle at the moment.

"I'm going to grab that shower now." She flattened the picture to her chest and started walking backward. "Have a seat. Relax. I'll be back soon."

Escaping to her bedroom, she closed the door behind her and paused to look at the photograph again.

Did it mean something that he'd never been far from her? Even through all those years spent apart?

With a groan, she tossed the photo onto the bed, grabbed her robe and headed for the shower. Once under the hot spray, she took the time to shave her legs, telling herself she would've done that anyway. Same with lathering on body lotion from head to toe after she dried off. And trying on five different sweaters before going with her first choice of a soft green V-neck cashmere pullover.

As normal as finding herself swiping on a light

coat of mascara and lip gloss after blowing dry her hair.

Yeah. Normal.

Nothing about today felt normal, nothing about the past week felt normal, but Leeann liked that. Grabbing her jacket and purse, she walked back into the living room.

Bobby stood. "Ready to hit the road?"

"Sure, let's go."

Minutes later, they were cruising the back roads outside of Destiny, enjoying the beautiful October afternoon with the sun shining down on them and the vibrant autumn trees whizzing by.

"Seems like old times, huh?" Bobby asked.

"As long as you've curbed your need for speed," Leeann replied, remembering the heart-stopping races from their teen years.

"Naw, never." Bobby shot her a grin. "But not in this sweet ride and not against doctor's orders."

He soon found a radio station that played the

oldies and it wasn't long before he had Leeann laughing as he sang along with Elvis.

"Maybe I shouldn't give up my day job, huh?" he asked.

"Probably not," she agreed, not sure what exactly his day job was anymore. "But the good thing is, no one heard you but me."

"Ouch!"

"Sorry, did your fragile ego take a direct hit?"

"I think it'll survive."

She leaned over and turned down the music. "How about telling me why you got me out here on the open road, as you put it."

He glanced over at her for a quick moment. "Maybe I just wanted to spend some time with you."

"We've been together every day for the last week," she said, pointing out the obvious, but liking how his words warmed her.

"Is that a problem?"

"No, of course not. Now, stop stalling. You said you had something you wanted to tell me."

He slowed the car, making it easier for them to talk. "I was wondering if you've given any thought to merging your land with the area set aside for the camp."

Stunned, Leeann only stared at him.

"I know you've always called it a pond, but actually it's a natural spring-fed lake. We both know from experience it's great for swimming and there's plenty of room for docks for smaller sailboats or kayaks. I mean, what's a summer camp without access to water, right?"

His suggestion made perfect sense. By combining the two parcels of land the camp would gain another eight acres. Bobby was right. What kid wanted to spend a week or two at a camp that didn't have swimming?

But did that mean he wanted her to sell him the land? Or was he looking at making her contribution to the camp a more permanent situation, meaning she would work for him?

Had Bobby decided to make the camp a reality?

"Maybe it wasn't such a good idea." He shrugged, breaking into her thoughts.

"No, I didn't say that." Leeann cut him off. "You just surprised me."

"So, you'll think about it? I don't want you to feel pressured into deciding anything right now."

Leeann nodded, and they continued their drive in silence until she noticed they were back on the road that led to town.

Was he taking her home? She didn't want this day to be over yet. "Is this the end of the ride?"

Bobby eased to a stop at the intersection. "Not if you don't want it to be. I thought we'd grab a pizza and take it back to my house."

Like a date?

Leeann pushed the thought from her head. "That sounds like a good idea. If I remember correctly we ended yesterday's meeting debating if the boys and girls cabins needed to be located at either end of the camp."

"Yeah, that's what we were talking about." His

hands tightened for a moment on the steering wheel. "I still don't think it matters."

"Do you have any memories of being a teenager?"

"Oh, yeah."

Leeann ignored the fluttering of her heart and reached into her purse for her cell phone. "Then, yes, the cabins need to be as far apart as possible."

"Where there's a will, there's a way." Bobby looked at her. "Unless you don't have any memories of being a teenager yourself?"

No, she remembered. All too well.

"I'll call in an order to Tony's. Does it matter what kind of pizza for Dean?"

The light changed to green and he hit the gas. "He's got a date with Katie Ledbetter this afternoon. I doubt he'll be at the house when we get there."

Bobby had no idea what his next move should be.

They arrived at his place just as fat raindrops

started to fall. Thankfully they got themselves and his T-bird into the garage before they got wet. Leeann had said little on the way home after picking up the pizza, but he'd seen her staring at the empty spot in the garage that normally held the pickup truck.

As he'd expected, they found no one home but a hungry Daisy and a note from Zip stating they were on their own for any camp discussion and to play nice together.

Words to live by.

He started the fire in the great room as darkness fell. Then the skies opened up and the rain came down in buckets. When Leeann suggested they eat by the fire, picnic-style, using a tablecloth she'd found in a kitchen drawer for a blanket, he thought it was a great idea.

Grabbing a bottle of wine, he clicked on the stereo and found that same oldies station they'd listened to in the car. They split the pizza, with an ever-watchful Daisy sitting nearby, and talked. About the weather, how much Destiny had grown and changed over the years, her collection of teapots and his art collection, anything but the camp.

Or their past.

Did he want to go down that road? Was it necessary?

He liked being with Leeann again, adult to adult. She was smart and beautiful and passionate about what mattered in her life. All the same things he'd fallen in love with as a boy, he appreciated in her as a woman.

A woman who had a secret.

He didn't know what that secret was—hell, he hated to speculate what it might be—but he couldn't ignore the signs.

Like that day in the Youth Center when her deputy friend had grabbed her and she'd put him down with ease.

"Come on, come and get it."

Leeann's persuasive tone cut into his thoughts.

She held out a piece of pizza topping. "Oh, come on, Daisy, I can tell you want this."

He grinned at her continued attempts to get along with the dog, who stood stiff-legged as she stared at the offering. "Of course she wants it. But I think it's a battle of wills, and Daiz is a stubborn girl."

"Here, you give it to her." Leeann sighed and handed over the offering. "Is it strange that I want her to like me?"

"I like you. Does that count?" He tossed the pepperoni at the dog, who gobbled it up. "Besides, she plays with the toys you've brought her. Just not when you're around to see it."

"Really?" Her face lit up with that fabulous smile of hers. "So, this is all just for show?"

He leaned back against the couch and laid his arm across the bottom cushions, his hand almost touching her shoulder. "I guess she just needs time to trust you."

Lee's smile faded. She didn't look sad exactly as she watched Daisy leave the room, but more like she understood where the animal was coming from. "So, where is she going now?"

"Hear that?" Bobby paused, and the sound of Daisy's nails on the hardwood floor slowly faded. "She's gone downstairs to Zip's bedroom to wait for him to come home."

"That's sweet."

Bobby turned his wrist and glanced at his watch. Knowing Zip, and the fact he'd been out with Katie twice already this week, the dog probably had a pretty long wait.

His cell phone vibrated in his pants pocket. Digging for it, Bobby looked at the screen. Speak of the devil. He pressed a button. "Hey, Zip."

Leeann rose, taking their plates and the almost-empty pizza box with her. "I'll take these into the kitchen."

"You don't have to—"

"That's okay. I'll be back in a minute."

Bobby watched her walk away, missing everything Zip said until he heard him mention something about a washout. "What—wait a minute, is the storm that bad?"

Bad enough that Zip was staying in town.

Leeann came back into the room and sat again as Bobby ended the call. He refilled their wine-glasses and handed Lee's to her. "Looks like this storm is wreaking havoc out there."

A crashing boom of thunder proved him right.

"Oh!" Leeann jumped, her wine sloshing in her glass.

Bobby slid closer, wrapping one arm around her shoulder. She flinched and he didn't know if that was from his touch or a second barrage from the storm. "Hey, it's okay. We're safe here."

"Is Dean on his way home?"

Was that panic in her voice? "He's staying wherever he is. The roads are a mess and there's no way he's going to try to drive." Bobby pulled in a deep breath, resting the hand holding his wineglass on his bent knee. "So it looks like you're going to be crashing here tonight."

That news caused Leeann to take a quick sip from her glass.

"Don't worry. There are three guest bedrooms

for you to choose from. I'll even loan you a T-shirt to sleep in."

Amazed at how calm his voice sounded, compared to the wild thumping of his heart at the idea of him and Leeann having the rest of the night together, Bobby paused to take a healthy swallow of wine.

Leeann stared into her glass for a moment, then gently placed it on the nearby coffee table before scooting even closer to him. "Can I…can I ask you a favor?"

Her voice was soft, her words hesitant.

Anything.

She could ask him anything and he'd move heaven and earth to make it happen. "Of course."

"Would you kiss me?"

Her request ratcheted up the sensual awareness he'd already had going on, of her scent, of the warmth of her skin. A need curled deep inside as he looked down at her upturned face. He lowered his head an inch, and watched her eyes widen and her lips part.

Would he kiss her?

Would he take the checked flag at the Daytona 500?

Maybe that was just wishful thinking but this kiss wasn't…

He had to do this right. He couldn't explain how he knew, but this moment meant something to Leeann. To them.

"Are you sure that's what you want?"

Asking her that, giving her the chance to back away took all the control he possessed, but she nodded, her gaze locked with his until his lips brushed hers.

Then her eyelids fluttered closed, her mouth hesitant and awkward beneath his. He closed his eyes, too, angling his head to fully claim the kiss, his hand rising to the silky smoothness of her hair.

Leeann stiffened and a soft cry escaped.

Dropping his hand, Bobby backed off and opened his eyes to find her chin trembling as she captured her lower lip in her teeth. A tear escaped from her still-closed eyes.

His gut twisted and he feared his assumptions about her secret were right.

"Lee…what is it? Tell me, please."

Chapter Ten

"S-six years ago, I was a-attacked on a photo shoot."

Leeann kept her eyes closed, her words hollow and soulless. There was no gentle lead-in, no protesting that she didn't know what Bobby was asking of her.

His only reaction to her statement was a swift intake of breath and a low mutter of a single curse.

People grew and changed while they were apart. Life and experience shaped who they were as adults. Somehow, Bobby had figured out there was something more to her history than just career changes and new relationships.

But spending time with him again had led to the reawakening of naive emotions from a first love and the unexpected transformation of those feelings to what she was experiencing now.

Leeann covered her face with her hands. A deep shuddering breath filled her chest as she fought to rein in her scattered thoughts and strewn feelings.

Here and now.

Concentrate on what is happening right here, right now.

She brushed away her tears, dragged her fingers over her cheeks until they curled into fists, one hand wrapped over the other, both pressed against her mouth.

Had she wanted Bobby to kiss her?

More than her next breath.

The longing had swelled from deep within her the moment he'd touched her shoulder to sooth her reaction to the storm. The sudden need surprised her, and she'd hoped the wanting would be enough to allow her to move past her emotional scars.

It wasn't.

She'd known that the moment he'd touched her hair.

Leeann's hands fell to her lap. Another deep breath, this one smooth and more controlled. If she ever wanted to be close to someone again, to be in a relationship again, the sharing of her past was a necessity.

Never had she dreamed it would be with Bobby.

"Lee, if you don't want to talk about this—"

"I do." Her voice was strong, even as her eyes stayed closed. "I want—I need to tell you if you're willing to listen."

"I'm right here."

She knew that. She could feel his presence, his strength as she started to speak. "It'd been a long day, the shoot had lasted for hours. Even though it had gotten dark outside, they…they still needed a few close-up shots of my mouth and hands. Most everyone was gone, including the photographer, who had another call. Just his assistant was there to take the last photographs, and a couple of the crew…and me."

The need to see Bobby, to know he was there, even if she couldn't look at him directly, made Leeann force her eyes open.

He wasn't touching her, but had placed his wineglass on the table, his hand wrapped around the stem, knuckles showing. His eyes were locked onto the fireplace, but other than a slight muscle tic at his jawline, there was no reaction from him.

"It was an international ad for some kind of alcohol. I had to keep pretending to drink…it was only water in the glass, but they kept refilling it…."

He turned to her and she paused, lowering her gaze to his leg. The tiny rip in his jeans at his knee commanded her full attention.

"To this day I don't remember leaving the studio that night. I learned later that the taxi driver had pulled up to my building and told the doorman he had a drunk in the backseat. They got me into the elevator and I must've had a moment of lucidity because I got inside my apartment. Took a shower... Hot, scalding water...my skin was so red. Then I passed out... for a second time."

The events of that night flashed in front of her eyes like a bad movie, but she watched and recited the details. The years and her recovery acted as a buffer between then and now.

"A few days later I started to remember...I realized what had happened. It came back in small flashes. Hands grabbing me, touching me..."

Tucking her legs tighter beneath her, she pressed against the warm leather of the couch, liking the security of its weight at her back. Her shoulders brushed against Bobby's arm, still lying across the bottom cushions. His unintentional embrace also felt safe and secure.

"I didn't want—despite how out of it I was, a part of me didn't like what was happening to me. I remember trying to push him away, to get away…."

This time she looked up at Bobby's face. A bright sheen of tears shined in his eyes. What did they mean? What did he see when he looked at her?

Right now that didn't matter. The only important thing was finishing her story. Get to the end, to where and who she was today. Then she'd deal with whatever came next.

One step at a time.

"You remember my long hair, right?" she asked, unable to stop herself from tucking the now short strands behind one ear.

He nodded.

"My hair was my trademark. It set me apart from the crowd. The long length could be manipulated in so many ways." She averted her gaze again, but kept her head high, staring at a spot on the wall over his shoulder. "He…used it to hold on to me. At one point I freed myself, but my hair was so long. He grabbed it and twisted it around his fist...I couldn't get away."

The helplessness she felt that night, and for months afterward, started to form inside her. Leeann pulled in several deep breaths and reminded herself of where she was and who she was with.

She was with Bobby, in his home. Safe. She was here because she wanted to be. Telling her story because she wanted to...needing to share her past with him.

No matter how it affected the future.

"I went to the police and they investigated. The conclusion was that I had been slipped Rohypnol, a drug used often in these kind of cases, but there was no medical proof because so much time had passed—I wasn't even positive who my attacker was. Eventually the case was dropped due to lack of evidence."

She sighed. "News that I didn't take very well. I turned into a recluse, not leaving my apartment. Things were bad…until Ursula found me. My folks had died in a car accident about six months before all this happened and my aunt worried when she couldn't reach me. She came to New York, rescued me and took me out of the city."

"You came home?" Bobby asked, his voice low and warm and so familiar it wrapped around her like a warm blanket. "You came back to Destiny?"

She shook her head. "No, this small town was the last place I wanted to be. Ursula understood that. She took me to stay with a professor friend of hers who lived outside of Chicago. I was quite a mess, but they got me the professional help I needed. I left my career behind and concentrated on healing and finding a way to live my life."

"And you've done that."

She nodded, looking at him again. The tears were gone from his eyes. In their place was a calm acceptance that encouraged her to go on. "Knowing I was in good hands, Aunt Ursula returned home. She had a business to run. But even the fire that destroyed my family's house a year later couldn't get me back to Destiny. I stayed in Chicago and concentrated on finishing my degree. Then four years ago—partly because of what happened to me—I made the choice to go into law enforcement, so I attended the Wyoming Law Enforcement Academy."

"But you said you didn't want to come home?"

"Ursula got sick." She dropped his gaze, her fingers tugging at the hem of her sweater. "It turned out to be cancer. She needed me to help her this time, so I completed the training, moved back home and applied for a job as a deputy sheriff in town. This is where I've been ever since."

She stopped talking, allowing the sounds of the room to fill the air: the soft ballad from the radio, the steady rain beating against the glass and the man next to her, breathing deep and low.

"Can I ask a question?"

Refusing to let the fear of whatever Bobby might say stop her, she nodded. "Of course."

"Can I hold you?" His arms remained open as he straightened his legs, creating space between them. "Would that be okay with you?"

Tears threatened again. Leeann had to bite hard at her bottom lip to hold back a sob. She jerked her head in a quick nod and flew into his arms. Clutching at his shirt, she willed back the tears as his heart pounded beneath her ear. A deep inhale filled her with his clean scent.

Thank you, thank you, thank you. The words echoed in her head, her heart. *Thank you for not turning away from me.*

"You're amazing, do you know that?"

She shook her head. "No, I'm not—"

The gentle pressure from his arms tightening around her stopped her protest.

"For once don't argue with me." His tone was teasing yet tender. "You are an amazing woman."

"Because of all I've gone through?" she asked.

"Because of all you've accomplished."

Leeann relaxed her grip on his shirt and settled fully into his arms. The strength of his embrace, warm and solid, enveloped her as she buried her face in his chest.

She had more to say, but for now she let the rise and fall of his breathing provide a steadying rhythm she clung to, her gaze centered on the dancing flames of the fireplace.

They sat in silence and listened to the rain, listened to each other breathing, and for the first time in a long time, a sense of peace settled over her.

The gentle chimes of a clock sounded twice before Leeann realized she had no idea how long they'd been sitting there.

"Oh, your back." She pushed away from him. "Why didn't you say anything? You must be in so much pain."

He released her with a smile. "Not so much. Just a bit stiff and sore from being on the floor."

She scrambled to her feet with a groan. "Do you need any help standing up?"

"You better back up a few steps." Bobby waved her off. "In case I end up flat on my face."

He didn't even sway as he got to his feet.

Daisy trotted into the living room. She circled Bobby's legs before continuing to the glass door and sat, looking up at him expectantly.

"It looks like someone needs to go outside. I'll be back in a few minutes."

Bobby disappeared with the dog and Leeann cleaned up the remains of their dinner. She quickly washed the few dishes they'd dirtied, straightened the coffee table and folded the tablecloth. Except for the fire, the room looked as if nothing profound had happened here tonight.

But Leeann knew that wasn't true.

"Well, Daisy is damp, but happy." Bobby returned alone, his hands full. "Here, I brought you something to sleep in. I'm sure you'll find a toothbrush and whatever else you might need in the guest bathroom."

Taking the clothing, she guessed their evening together had come to an end. It was probably for the best. Emotionally exhausted, she could only guess what must be running through Bobby's head. "Thanks."

He walked her to one of the bedrooms at the opposite end of the house from his room. She tossed the clothing on the bed, not surprised when she turned around and found he hadn't stepped over the threshold.

"You okay?" he asked.

Not really, but she'd unloaded enough on him tonight.

Leeann crossed her arms over her chest and walked back to the doorway. There was still something she needed to say. "I owe you an apology."

"No, you don't."

"Please." She waved one hand at him. "Let me say this."

Bobby nodded and remained silent.

"I realized…even before tonight…that part of my recovery from—well, from that event—occurred because I could compartmentalize my life into before and after. Before being everything connected with my life in New York and after being…everything that came after." She dropped her hands. "Even in the few years I've been back in town I was able to separate my life here in Destiny into before and after."

"Then I came back."

It was as if he'd read her mind. "Suddenly the walls I'd built that kept you firmly in my past crumbled…and I started to play the 'what if' game. You know, what if I hadn't left town, hadn't left you…."

Her voice trembled and she pressed her fingers to her lips for a moment. The compassion in his eyes almost caused her to release what little control she had left. "And instead of dealing with those questions, I lashed out at you. Picking on everything from your home to your career, even your health, just so I wouldn't have to face…"

"It's okay, Lee. I understand."

She gripped the door with one hand and braced the other against the wall, her knees suddenly weak. "I was afraid telling you would…change things between us." She forced the question from her lips because she had to know. "Has it?"

Bobby's jaw clenched for a moment then he said, "Yeah, I think so."

Her heart dropped. "I see."

"No, Lee…wait." He reached out, his calloused fingers brushing along her chin. "Everything we've learned about each other, about our pasts, the good and the bad, over the last couple of weeks has led us to where we are right now. But that doesn't mean I've changed my mind about spending time with you. Talking, laughing, touching…kissing."

The breath disappearing from her lungs. "You still want—you want to kiss me?"

"Oh, yeah."

The longing in his voice both thrilled and worried her, but in a good way. Would he kiss her now? Should she reach out to him? Uncertainty kept her motionless as silence stretched between them.

Finally Bobby dropped his hand and took a step back, breaking the spell woven between them.

"Good night, Lee."

She nodded and closed the door. Willing herself not to cry, she refused to allow her disappointment to fall over the edge into rejection.

Quickly undressing, Leeann pulled on the large T-shirt, knowing the sweatpants he'd given her would never stay up. Face washed and teeth brushed, she slipped between the cool sheets. The bedside clock read eleven o'clock. She closed her eyes and tried to give in to the exhaustion.

Three hours later, she was still wide awake.

After finally figuring out the remote control for the flat-screen television, she couldn't find anything but infomercials, repeats of eighties sitcoms and a black-and-white movie version of *Pride and Prejudice* that hit a little too close to home.

A sudden need for a cup of hot tea had Leeann crawling out of bed.

Opening the bedroom door, she strained to hear any signs that Bobby might still be up and moving around, but silence greeted her and she made her way to the kitchen. Minutes later, she hit the button on the microwave to release the door before the buzzer sounded. She quickly dunked the tea bag then sipped at the strong, hot liquid. Straight, no milk, lemon or sugar.

Already she felt better.

Padding barefoot across the family room, she stood in front of the floor-to-ceiling glass wall, drank her tea and got lost in the sound of the rain still coming down until—

Was that a moan?

Spinning around, she quickly moved into the living room. She waited. Listening. Maybe she'd been wrong. No, the sound came again, longer and louder, it echoed down the hallway that led to the master bedroom.

Without pausing to consider if she should,

Leeann placed the mug on the fireplace mantel and turned the corner. When she reached Bobby's partially open bedroom door, a faint light flickered inside. It had to be from a television.

Maybe that's what she heard.

No, there it was again. It was him.

She crept closer. Was he awake? In pain? She peeked inside, her eyes immediately drawn to the king-size bed against the far wall and the man writhing beneath the covers.

"Bobby?"

His only response was another deep groan.

She hurried across the room to the side of the bed where he laid, eyes squeezed closed as his head rocked back and forth against the pillows. His legs scissored beneath the blankets, which gathered low at his waist.

"Got to…got to get out…" His words burst from his mouth as his hand clawed at air.

Oh, God, he was in the middle of a nightmare. Should she try to wake him? She couldn't leave him like this.

"Got to get to Lee…"

The anguish in his voice as he said her name tore at her heart. Was he dreaming about her? Had she caused this by telling him what had happened? She'd certainly experienced her own share of nightmares about that night.

"Bobby, can you hear me? Please, you need to wake up."

His tightly shut eyes and incoherent mutterings told her that he was still lost in his nightmare.

She had to do something to help.

Leaning over, she gently placed one hand on his bare biceps. The muscles bunched beneath her touch. "Bobby, please."

In a heartbeat, he grabbed her and yanked her against his chest. She cried out, reaching for his shoulders, missing and landing hard on top of him. He instinctively rolled, trapping her beneath him.

Panic flooded her veins, trading logic and reason with immobilizing fear. Instinctively, she struggled to wiggle free, but his sheet-covered legs pinned hers in place, his hips molding perfectly in line to hers.

"Bobby, it's me. It's Leeann."

Saying the words aloud helped her to remember where she was and who was holding her down. She repeated them again and again, her terror fading when she curved her arms around his waist. The weight of him was heavy, yet familiar even after all these years.

His hold on her shoulders lightened when she touched him, but then his head dipped to the curve of her neck.

"Lee..." He whispered her name again, his breath ragged and hot against her skin.

Pinpricks of pleasure danced across her skin, causing her to shiver. With delight, not fear. Elation centered in her chest then splintered into a million pieces filling every inch of her.

Instinct now had her pressing closer to him. "Yes, it's me. Wake up, Bobby, you're dreaming, but it's okay. I'm right here with you."

* * *

He was going to die.

Bobby's hands tightened on the steering wheel as he struggled to control the careening mess of twisted metal that used to be his race car. Other drivers flew by in a vivid and dazzling array of bright colors while the screech of tires and clang of crushed sheet metal pounded in his head.

The pungent stink of burned rubber and the stomach-heaving stench of gasoline filled his nose. Thick dark smoke made it impossible to see. Seconds later, he was airborne, twisting and flipping, the harness and safety belt holding his body in place.

Then a gust of wind cleared the air and he could see someone—a woman—standing in the middle of the track, oblivious to the racing machines screaming past her.

Leeann.

She stood there, smiling, her arms raised out to him, calling his name.

Was she crazy? She was going to be killed!

He had to get to her, keep her protected and safe from harm. Finally the upside-down motion stopped and he was on the ground, crawling across burning asphalt, dirt and rocks digging into his skin.

He reached her, pulled her into his arms and covered her, sheltering her body with his. The clean scent of her skin, her gentle touch, her words assuring him she was okay, pushed away his panic and fear.

"Bobby, it's okay, everything is all right."

Her words a warm whisper as her lips brushed against his ear, her soft curves pressed into the hard lines of his body. He opened his mouth to respond, but the temptation of her arched neck was too much to resist. Nipping lightly, he felt her answering shudder run the length of their bodies.

So real and yet he knew he was dreaming.

Unable to stop, he traced the curve of her jaw with his mouth, inching closer to the one reward he craved. Anticipation burned until her soft sigh welcomed him home. Then her hands urged him closer as he received a kiss from the one girl he'd never forgotten.

This was what Bobby had dreamed of for years while laying in his army bunk, then a waterbed at his lakeside condo and more recently a hospital bed.

What a sweet dream it was.

Leeann back in his arms, returning kisses that held the faint nostalgia of their youth, but also burned with the adult fire of renewed passion.

Slipping his arm around her shoulders, he leaned to one side, wanting the space to touch her, to kiss her, everywhere.

She moved a hand from his back to his face, angling her head as the kiss deepened and his tongue boldly swept over hers. His fingers trailed down the side of her body, grazing over one breast until they cupped the sexy curve of her hip.

Desire overrode caution, even if he wasn't

completely sure why they should be careful. Then she broke free with a soft moan that drove his mouth lower to leave wet kisses along her collarbone as he pushed aside the loose collar of her T-shirt.

One of her legs slipped between his, but all he felt was the cottony smoothness of the bed linen. He wanted—needed—to feel the smoothness of her skin. Releasing her waist, his hand dropped lower until he was rewarded with the warmth of her upper thigh. A memory of how ticklish she'd been returned, and his fingers lightly danced over her skin.

Her hand slid over his, curling around his wrist, then squeezing tight. "B-Bobby…"

Her trembling sigh went straight to his heart. Then his head.

The warm fuzziness disappeared with the shock of realizing he was awake. He stilled. This wasn't a dream. Leeann really was in his arms, in his bed.

But how? When had they—

Squeezing his eyes tight, he fought off the lingering effects of his nightmare and tried to remember how they'd ended up tangled in his sheets. Then her haunting words from just a few hours ago came back to him, twisting his gut. Bracing himself on his elbow, he backed off, hating the cool air that touched his skin even as she arched beneath him.

He twisted free of her hold on his wrist. "Lee, wait."

She went still before a shiver racked her body, vibrating through him where they laid pressed together.

Using every nasty cussword in his extensive vocabulary, Bobby silently berated himself for his stupidity and withdrew even farther, trying to bring his body's natural instincts back under control.

He grabbed the far edge of the comforter and pulled it over her. "We can't..." he said. "We shouldn't be doing this."

"Because you're awake now?" Leeann's words fell from her mouth in a hushed whisper.

He was handling this all wrong.

Never mind the fact he didn't have the slightest clue how he was supposed to handle a situation like this.

Bobby dropped back against the pillows and cushioned headboard, his arm still caught under her shoulders. He pulled her toward him, but she resisted.

"I'd like to hold you…and explain." If he could. Hell, his mind was so jumbled he wasn't sure what he was going to say. Or how his reasons for pulling away from her were going to come out. "If you'll let me."

He waited, not bothering to count. He'd stay here, just like this, for as long as it took. Finally, Leeann rolled toward him, stretching her long, lean body next to his, her head nestled on his shoulder. She brought her warmth and the quilted comforter with her, draping it over both of them.

Good thing, too. While his head and his heart told him what had just happened between them was too soon, certain parts of his body were having a tough time getting with the program.

Then he thought again about what she'd shared with him and his desire cooled, replaced by a burning need for retribution that was six years too late.

Revenge would do nothing to help Leeann now, so he pushed the feeling aside and gently wrapped his arm around her. "I can't explain what just happened. I didn't realize what I was doing. I'm sor—"

She reached up and laid a hand over his mouth. "The last thing I need right now is an apology."

Silence filled the air for a long moment before she withdrew her hand and tucked it beneath her own chin. "I couldn't sleep," she continued. "I heard you from the living room and realized you were having a bad dream. I tried to wake—"

"And I yanked you down and kissed you."

"And I kissed you back. So I don't understand what the problem is."

Bobby sighed and tried to gather his scattered thoughts before he spoke. Even so, he had a feeling this was going to come out wrong.

Chapter Eleven

"I don't think you're ready for this." He looked down and saw only the top of her head, her dark hair shining in the flickering light from the flat-screen television. "When I held you down with my body, you tried to get away from me."

That had been a guess, since he'd been lost in his own sweet dream then, but Leeann's continued silence told him he was right.

Pieces of his nightmare came back to him. He realized it was connected to what she'd share with him tonight. He wanted to save her from that horrific event, and yet when he actually had her in his arms, he let his need and desire override common decency.

He'd never felt more like a loser in his life.

"At first, yes, I was scared." Leeann's voice was soft, but clear. "You were dreaming…about me. You called out my name. So I concentrated on who was holding me and touching me… I know you weren't trying to hurt me."

Bobby closed his eyes when her warm breath brushed over his bare chest. She pressed against the length of his body, one long bare leg peeking out from the comforter to curl up over his. She was probably unaware of what she was doing, but her body heat steamed through the silky cotton sheet between them.

His libido started to respond again, but this wasn't the right time and it had nothing to do with her confession last night.

Okay, that was a lie, but he couldn't stay next to her and trust himself to keep his hands off her. He had no idea what it would mean if they made love again.

After all this time, after all they'd been through, were they just looking to re-create what they shared years ago? Was Leeann even ready for a physical relationship?

With him, of all people?

With so much of his life still undecided, like whether he could get his racing career back on track or if he should invest in this crazy summer-camp idea, Bobby didn't have anything to offer Leeann.

He couldn't have just a no-strings-attached fling with her. Not with the woman he once planned to spend the rest of his life with. If they did start something, were they just heading for a bigger crash than the one he'd experienced six months ago?

He honestly didn't know if he could survive that.

"Is my past too much to deal with?" Lee's voice cut through his thoughts. "I haven't been intimate with anyone since the attack. A few dates, here and there, but it never went anywhere. Wrong time, wrong men, I don't know...I guess it was just me."

He gave her shoulder a gentle squeeze. "It's not you."

"I thought because of our history together and how great these last couple week have been—"

Her voice broke and Bobby was sure she'd choked back a sob.

"Lee, I just told you, it's not you."

"Stop saying that!" She shook her head against his chest and he felt her tears on his skin. "Please just tell me the truth."

She wanted the truth, fine, but he wanted to see her face, to look into her eyes and know she believed him when he told her. Placing his hands on her hair, he started to tilt her up to face him. Leeann flinched and cried out. He immediately let go, realizing what he'd done when her fingers frantically brushed over the short strands.

"Lee, I'm sorry." A dull ache sat hard in his

stomach as he watched her movements. "I didn't mean to scare you."

"You didn't." She rose, propping herself on one arm, her head bent and her hair hiding her face. "My h-hair got caught in your watch."

He looked at his wrist, his heart twisting into a tight knot when he saw the dark strands caught in the watchband he'd forgotten to remove last night. Yanking it off, he tossed the watch to his bedside table.

Except for getting Leeann to come back here for dinner, nothing about this night was going as planned. Hell, except for his physical therapy, nothing had since he arrived in town. A part of him had known being back in Destiny was going to be hard, but reconnecting with Leeann in ways he never thought possible was reawakening old and surprisingly painful memories.

"Losing you devastated me."

She finally looked at him.

"When you ended things." Bobby paused, wanting to make sure Lee wasn't crying. Her eyes were wide with surprise, but dry. "When you walked away from everything, I thought my world had come to an end."

Leeann nodded. "Graduation was the next day and it was all such a blur, I don't really remember much of it."

"If it wasn't for my mother, I probably wouldn't have even gone to the ceremony. I stayed long enough to grab my diploma, then Justin and I took off for an old hunting cabin with a case of beer and a few bottles of Jack."

"And I headed to New York the next day. I…I thought you would come after me."

"Me, you and your parents in the Big Apple?"

"They didn't—I told them to stay home. My prize included a furnished apartment for a month and the chance to secure a modeling contract, which I did within the first couple of weeks. I was determined to make it on my own."

Now he was the one who was surprised. "Lee, I had to report to the army two weeks after graduation."

She gave a halfhearted shrug. "Still, there was two weeks."

"You threw the ring at my head."

"I know, I remember." Leeann closed her eyes for a moment. "I guess I really wanted you to be happy for me, to share in what I wanted to do. Boy, it sounds as crazy now for me to say that as it was for me to think that way back then."

Bobby sighed and tunneled his fingers through his hair. "Yeah, well, I spent most of those fourteen days drunk off my ass. Thankfully, the following months in boot camp and training saved me. I ate, lived and breathed the army so I could get over—"

"Over me." She finished his sentence, her hands tightly fisted around the blanket in her lap. "Oh, Bobby, I never realized…we were so young. So in love. So sure what we were planning was the right thing, but then I got scared. The closer we got to June, the more I realized I was trading one safe world for another."

"And you didn't want safe?"

"I was eighteen years old. I badly wanted out from under my parents' control. Being with you was fun and passionate…and crazy. It took me a long time to figure out I'd really run from my folks as much as I ran from you and your engagement ring. Winning that modeling contest gave me a chance at being my own person, to be independent, and I had to grab that chance. Can you understand that?"

Bobby jerked his head in a quick nod and slid out of bed.

"Wait, are you the one running away now?"

Grabbing a pair of sweatpants, he yanked them on over his briefs. "No, I just need to get up and move around a bit."

"Oh, are you in pain?"

He had some faint twinges as he moved so it wasn't a total lie, but he latched on to her excuse. "Yeah, my back is bothering me a bit."

Facing the window, he saw the storm had passed and only a light rain continued to fall.

Slowly stretching his muscles, he was conscious of Leeann's gaze on him.

"You've gained back the weight you lost." Her voice carried across the room. "*People* magazine will be calling you for their Most Eligible Bachelors issue again."

He spun around. "You saw that?"

She nodded, having moved to sit in the spot he'd abandoned, the blanket now covering her body. "Both times. Those Hollywood hunks had nothing on you."

"I doubt that, and it wasn't much compared to all your magazine appearances." He nudged the footstool from the chair in the nearby seating area closer to the bed and sat. "It seemed like I couldn't ever walk into the PX and not see your face staring back at me."

"PX?"

"Ah, post exchange. That's what they call the store on an army post. Sort of like a Wal-Mart for the military."

"Yes, I was very lucky with my modeling."

She released a deep sigh. "Luckier than most. In less than six months, I got my first magazine cover."

"I carried it around in my wallet for a long time."

Her gaze shot back at him. "You did not."

Bobby couldn't believe he'd just told her that. "Yeah, well, my buddies thought I was lying when I told them I used to date you."

"You told people about me? About us?"

Bobby leaned forward, his elbows on his knees, hands clasped between them. "Naw, not really. Just Zip."

"I use to look for you."

"Huh?"

Leeann snuggled down against his pillows and stretched out her legs, bare toes peeking out from the ends of the blanket. "After 9/11, I did a USO tour of military bases. I used to search a sea of camouflage, looking for your face. I hoped we might run into each other again."

He found he liked the idea of her looking for

him, even if it had been for nothing. "I was out of the army by then and living in North Carolina."

"Oh. Were you racing?"

"No, but I did luck out and got hired on a crew as a mechanic. It was another couple of years before I got behind the wheels of anything more than a piece of junk."

"Until you took over for an injured driver and won the first major race you drove in." She offered him a small smile. "I didn't find out about that until the following year when you started driving full-time and were on the news a lot. Your first win…well, that happened right around the time my life was imploding."

Her star had fallen just as his started to rise. Within a year of that race he had endorsement offers coming at him left and right. He'd worked hard at his career, both on the track and off, and it was another year or so before he realized he hadn't seen or heard anything about his former girlfriend. Until a late-night search on Google revealed her sudden retirement.

"Is it okay if I ask—" a long yawn interrupted her and she cover her mouth with the corner of the blanket until it passed "—if I ask you what happened to that ring? The one you gave me?"

"It's at the bottom of Diamond Lake."

She startled. "What?"

"Your pond out there?" He waved at the window, even though the body of water was on the other side of the house. "That's what I've always called it. The morning I left town, I stopped by and heaved the ring as close to the center as I could."

"So it's down at the bottom somewhere." Her eyelids fluttered a few times, then closed. "Hmm, I like the sound of that. Diamond Lake. You know, I've decided something. If you make a go of the camp, it's yours. You can have Diamond Lake."

Bobby's chest grew tight at her generous offer, even though he knew he'd never accept it. "Lee, you're half asleep. You don't know what you're saying."

Her eyes popped open and just like that, the flames of desire for this girl, for the woman she'd become, started licking again at his soul.

Her dark eyes, sleepy and sexy, stared straight into his. "I'm not asleep. I'm going back to my own bed in a minute and I know exactly what I'm saying. You're still mulling over the idea of making the summer-camp plans a reality, I get that, but if you do take that leap, I want those kids to know the magic of that wonderful place."

Her eyes slid closed again and he couldn't help but smile at the sight of her body settled deeper into his pillows and blankets.

"Do me one favor, okay?" Her words came out in a soft whisper. "Don't let anything happen to my bench."

The natural bench at the water's edge created by two fallen trees. Bobby knew the spot intimately. He first kissed Leeann there, held her in his arms more times than he could count as they sat and watched the seasons go by. He'd knelt before that same bench when he asked her to marry him all those years ago.

"I won't. I promise." He rose and walked again to the window. The dark night and rain made it impossible to see, but he knew what was out there. Acres and acres of some of the most beautiful land in the state of Wyoming. And he was going to make sure others knew that, too. "I'm going ahead with the camp."

The words popped out of his mouth and immediately he felt the rightness of what he just said. No matter what happened with his racing career, he wanted to build that camp and he wanted Leeann to help him.

"Lee? Did you hear what I said?" He turned to face her. "It might be crazy, but I'm going to—"

His words caught in his throat when he saw she'd rolled away, taking the blanket with her, leaving her back uncovered. His T-shirt hugged her curves but bunched around her waist displaying her perfect backside and her long, sleek and toned legs to his view. The word *Heartbreaker* was emblazoned in bold red letters across her bright pink cotton underwear.

He dropped into the closest chair.

It was either that or he was going to take the ten steps that would get him back to his bed and join her. What he should do is cover her, and leave. Find another bed. Goodness knows, the house had plenty of them, but he couldn't move.

He sat there, watching her, knowing they'd covered a lot of ground in talking about their past. Still, he was in awe by the fact she wanted to be in a physical relationship again, with him. But was that all she wanted?

Was that all he wanted? Was he going to be the one to break her heart this time?

Other than his just-made decision about the summer camp, he had no idea what his future held. Destiny was his hometown, but his life was in North Carolina with his race team. Yeah, they'd done okay without him this summer with a top-ten finish in the final standings, but that only meant he needed to make an assessment of his career plans.

"Where do I belong?" He spoke the words aloud and waited. Silence was his only answer.

Several hours later, Leeann entered Ursula's Updos, her aunt's beauty parlor located in the center of town. The shop was so busy, it took her fifteen minutes to get from the front door to her aunt's side.

"Can we talk?" She tugged on her aunt's sleeve and nodded toward the back of the shop. "I know it's Wacky Wednesday, but I really need to. It won't take long."

Ursula smiled around the bobby pins stuck between her lips and held up two fingers, forming a V, the universal peace sign. Leeann took that to mean her aunt still needed a couple more minutes to finishing twirling Ms. Dimpleton's gray locks into pin curls.

Yes, Wacky Wednesday, as her aunt had dubbed the busiest day of the week for her and her other stylists, was in full swing, all because Wednesday was bingo and chili night down at the fire station, where Devlin Murphy commanded the stage as he called out the bingo numbers.

Dev had the true heritage of an Irishman, a leprechaun's charm in a smoking-hot body. His way with the game of chance, and with the ladies no matter what age, was bringing them in from as far away as Cheyenne. Not that the volunteer fire department was complaining.

But the beauty parlor being so busy also meant Leeann had a lot of chatting and hellos to return.

Most of the ladies asked about her plans now that she was no longer employed by the sheriff's department. A few, including Ms. Dimpleton, who showed off her Winslow pride by wearing a sweatshirt emblazoned with Bobby's image, had been bold enough to bring up her and Bobby's past, noting she still remembered how they used to run around together as teenagers.

Pushing aside the memories caused by the

elderly woman's questions, Leeann dug deep for her best pageant smile and a vague reply, and managed to get through the inquiries relatively unscathed.

Grabbing a handful of green grapes from the basket of fresh fruit sitting on the front desk, Leeann headed for the back of the salon.

She propped open the side door that lead to a quiet alley, allowing the fumes from perms and hair dyes to escape. Last night's storm was long gone and another beautiful, warm fall day had arrived. A deep breath pulled in the mouthwatering smells of Sherry's Diner from across the street.

Boy, she was hungry.

She'd refused Bobby's offer of breakfast that morning because she'd wanted to get out of the house before Dean returned home. She'd asked him to drive her home soon after they woke up.

With her alone in his bed and him sprawled in a nearby chair.

Now it was almost noon and she still hadn't

eaten. Popping a grape in her mouth, she tried not to think about the past twenty-four hours.

It was impossible.

She'd fallen asleep last night, actually very early this morning, wrapped in the warmth of Bobby's comforter even after she'd decided it'd be best for both of them if she went back to the guest bedroom.

Instead she ended up staying right where she was with Bobby's reasons for ending the kisses and touches between them echoing in her head.

This shouldn't be happening right now.

I didn't realize what I was doing.

You've been through enough tonight.

Every one made sense and, yes, she'd been nervous and jumpy, and altogether unsure of what she was doing, but six—no, more like seven years of celibacy could do that to a person.

No matter what happened in the past.

Then there had been the talk about their history, a much needed clearing of the air after all these years. She had to admit it felt good to talk about their old relationship with the observations of some hard-learned lessons and a growing maturity from adulthood.

So why did she still feel so lost?

"Whew, we are hopping today." Ursula stepped through the doorway fanning herself with a celebrity gossip magazine. "God bless Devlin Murphy! If I was a little younger I'd show him just how much I appreciate all the business he brings me!"

Leeann smiled. It was great to see her aunt, who reminded her of Jamie Lee Curtis with her tall, lean frame, short spiky hair artfully colored a deep brunette and a half-dozen gold hoop earrings dangling from her left earlobe. Ursula had recovered from cancer twice in the past three years, and she was back to her normal, wise-cracking, hairstyling self.

"Now." Her aunt dropped into one of the metal chairs clustered around a small table the girls used during their breaks. "Tell me what's got you so upset."

"What makes you think I'm upset?"

"It's written all over your face, honey. Let me guess…it has something to do with Bobby."

Leeann opened her mouth to protest, but it was useless.

She plopped down and spilled everything that'd happened over the past few weeks, right up to last night when she woke Bobby from his nightmare and his passionate response.

Her words came in a nonstop flow until she ended with a deep sigh and admitted, "And I have absolutely no idea what I should do now."

"Maybe doing nothing is the best thing. I know that's hard for you. You were always a planner, long before it became your way to deal with your past."

"So, the plan is to do…nothing?"

"Sweetie, you're trying to handle two different things at the same time—the 'will it or won't it happen' when it comes to the summer camp." Ursula paused, her voice dropping to a whisper. "Yes, I know that's supposed to be a secret. Don't worry, I haven't breathed a word to anyone."

"I think Bobby's going to build the camp."

Her aunt's face lit up with a bright smile, then it quickly faded. "You think?"

"We didn't talk about it too much last night, except for me telling him if he does go ahead with the plan I'm going to give him my land to be added to the total acreage."

"That doesn't surprise me," Ursula said. "But you're still not sure if he's going to do this?"

"I was half asleep and I'm afraid I only heard what I wanted to hear." She sighed. "And this morning I couldn't bring myself to ask him outright."

"Afraid of what the answer might be?"

"About so many things." Leeann paused, then licked her lips. "He kissed me. Really kissed me. I panicked at first, but then I was enjoying being in his arms, but he stopped...said I wasn't ready to be intimate with him. Maybe he's right."

"Maybe *he's* the one who's not ready." Ursula

reached across the table and took Leeann's hand in her own. "I agree that talking about your breakup was long overdue, but that's only one of the two pretty big conversations you had last night.

"You need to remember, you've had six years and a whole lot of therapy to deal with your past. Bobby has had less than a day. Remember when you told me how Racy and Maggie reacted to your news? How you ended up reassuring and comforting them during your girls' weekend? To you, what happened in New York is something you've moved on from, but to your friends, and now to Bobby—"

"It's still brand-new. Yes, he mentioned something like that last night. After he stopped kissing me."

"So, give him time to come to terms with your past. Then you two can decide if what you're feeling for each other involves something more than just friendship."

Leeann sighed. "Maybe that's just it. Maybe

getting involved with Bobby again isn't the right thing. I have no idea what his future plans are, no matter what he decides about the camp. He's made it quite clear these last few weeks that he has every intention of going back to racing."

"Could that be because he doesn't have anything else waiting for him? Like you?"

Leeann had never considered that. Bobby had his home, family and plenty of friends in Destiny. Did he want her, too?

"You know, for whatever reason, the universe has destined that the two of you are back in each other's lives." Her aunt, always a bit of a free spirit, offered a smile that spoke of years of experience. "Maybe someone up there is trying to tell you both that it's time to take a chance again."

Leeann remained silent, unsure of how to respond. Unsure if she had it in her to love Bobby again. To love anyone.

"Think about what I said." Ursula rose. "Come

on, I need to make sure Ms. Dimpleton's pin curls haven't turned her into Medusa."

They walked back into the beauty parlor together and Leeann gave her aunt a peck on the cheek before heading for the front door. As she reached for the handle, Fay Coggen entered carrying a large, rectangular box in her hands.

"Hey, there." Leeann stepped back to allow the local florist, whose shop was just a few doors away, to come inside. "Don't tell me you're making personal deliveries now?"

Fay glanced toward the doorway for a moment, her smile a bit wobbly. "No, but the man who was going to deliver—well, my delivery guy had to run another errand so I thought I'd bring these myself."

"So who are they for?" Leeann asked when Ursula joined them. "Have you got one of those cute doctors from the hospital courting you, Auntie?"

Ursula laughed as Fay cleared her throat and said, "No, actually, they're for you."

Shocked, Leeann could only stand there as the florist placed the box in her hands. "Me?"

"I was going to drop them off at your house, but I saw your car parked out front so...here they are."

The packed salon went silent. Unable to think of a way to gracefully get out of opening the box in front of everyone, Leeann laid it on the counter and lifted the lid.

Brushing aside the green tissue paper, she found a stunning mixture of deep blue-purple stalks and vivid long-stemmed yellow roses. The ladies offered oohs and ahhhs, but Leeann was speechless. She looked at her aunt, who only smiled and offered her a quick wink.

"Wow." Leeann struggled to put her thoughts into words. "They're beautiful. What are... where..."

"These are Blue Mountain Gladiolus. They symbolize strength of character." Fay lightly caressed the flowers as she spoke. "And the yellow roses are for joy and friendship."

Leeann's fingers trembled as she lifted the small white envelope tucked among the flowers. She pulled out the card. In a dark, masculine scrawl it read, "Love, Bobby."

Chapter Twelve

"What would you say if I told you I plan to build a summer camp for kids on my remaining land?"

"I'd say the Destiny gossip grapevine is alive and well." Valzora Winslow smiled up at her son after she returned his welcome-home hug. "And has gone international."

They stood in the middle of his mother's living room, which looked like a luggage shop that had exploded, with the variety of bags, totes and cases strewn everywhere. She had called a little while ago to say she was on her way back home from the airport in Cheyenne.

Two days early.

He'd put aside the contracts he'd been reviewing all afternoon, not that he was making any progress anyway. Stopping at the local florist shop for the second time today, he made it to his mother's place just as the car service limo departed.

His mother's response stunned him. "You've been back in town, what? Twenty minutes? How did you know anything about the camp? This is supposed to be a secret, by the way."

"Oh, honey, nothing in this town is secret for very long." She pulled her cell phone from her pocket. "You know, I just love this little gadget you got me before I left for my cruise. Have you ever tried texting? Or maybe I mean tweeting? It takes some learning, but it's amazing what a person can say in less than a hundred and forty characters."

Bobby couldn't believe it.

He barked out a laugh, feeling better than he had all day, and wrapped the petite woman in another big hug. Boy, he'd missed her.

After being with his mother every day for four months during his recovery, they'd grown close again. Back to "the two of us against the world" kind of relationship they'd had while he was growing up.

"Oh, you feel good and strong," she said. "I can tell Dean's been working you hard."

"He's been a slave driver, but it was worth it. I'm cane-free and back in the driver's seat."

"And the pain?"

He didn't bother to look away to try to hide anything from her. He never could. "It still flairs up from time to time, especially if I push myself too hard."

"Which you do on a regular basis, I'm sure." She eyed the bouquet of fall flowers in his hand. "Are those for me?"

"Yeah." Bobby handed over the flowers,

realizing he'd forgotten all about them. "Here you go."

"My, aren't they pretty! Come on, I'll get a vase for these. Do you want something to drink?" She headed for her cheery yellow kitchen. "I could use a cup of tea."

"Water would be great."

"Oh, thank heavens for my book club." His mother filled a glass with water and added a few ice cubes. "Fresh food in my refrigerator, my plants watered—"

"And your garden was taken care of." Bobby lifted the glass to his mouth and took a long swallow. "Thanks to Leeann."

"Yes." She sent him a quick wink. "I'm glad she had the time, seeing how busy she's been despite her current state of unemployment."

He shook his head. "Let me guess? You also already know she's been helping with the plans for the camp."

"Rumor is the idea for the camp was hers to start with."

In no time, she had the flowers artfully arranged in a vase in the middle of her table, and the kettle was heating on the stove. "So, tell me about this camp. Is it bringing back good memories from your own camp experiences?"

Bobby shared what he, Leeann and Zip had figured out so far when it came to buildings, layout and programs. He found himself wishing he'd brought the plans with him to show her all the work they'd done over the past couple of weeks.

"Sounds like you're excited about this project," his mother said when he finished.

"I am," he admitted, a bit surprised. "Getting my hands on that land was something I did because I finally had the means to fulfill a boisterous promise I made as a kid. I wanted to prove to this town, to Lee, that I was worthy of living there, that I had the money to build a home, even if I wasn't sure I'd ever stay in it full-time."

"But I thought you had plans to bring your racing operations here."

"Yeah, but again, I think I was looking at that proposal because it was something I could do financially, you know? Money was no object, but was it right? Then Lee puts this crazy idea in my head, something the whole town can get behind."

"Can I play the mother card and pry by asking if there are any lingering sparks between you two?"

"Between me and the girl you never approved of?"

"That was a long time ago, sweetie. You were too young to be in such a serious relationship, both of you." She rose and pulled her favorite tea mug from the cupboard and placed it on the counter. "Now you've both grown up, experienced life and, from the sounds of it, are spending quite a bit of time together. Is that a good thing?"

Bobby had no idea how to answer her.

Her tea mug reminded him of the one he'd seen Leeann grab off the fireplace mantel and place in the sink after she'd emerged from his guest bedroom, fully dressed, insisting she needed to get home.

That was about all she'd said after waking up in his bed.

He'd stayed awake, watching her sleep and finally allowed her haunting words about the attack to replay in his head. After dropping her off at home this morning, the horror of what she'd gone through dominated his thoughts.

Zip finally returned and found him doing laps in the pool. When his buddy asked how many he was up to, Bobby couldn't honestly give him an answer. Then he'd asked about Leeann, and Bobby only ducked beneath the water and started swimming again.

He couldn't stop himself from wondering how she was doing. Did she get the flowers yet? Having first planned to drop them off at her house himself, he'd left the shop and spotted her in a deep conversation with her aunt outside Ursula's shop.

Even from across the street, he could see she was upset so he decided to have the flowers delivered instead. Decided? More like chickened out. And unable to come up with the right words, as if there were any, he'd just scrawled his name on the card.

A piercing whistle broke into his thoughts.

"Sweetheart, what is it?" His mother grabbed the kettle and filled her mug with the steamy liquid. "You got lost in your own thoughts there for a moment. What's bothering you?"

Glossing over the details, Bobby told her about last night's dinner and what Leeann had shared with him about her past, knowing his mother would keep what he was saying in confidence.

Her sharp intake of breath and teary eyes conveyed her sorrow. "Oh, that poor girl, but I'm not surprised she's handled it the way she has. She was always strong, in body and spirit."

Bobby nodded in silent agreement, still amazed at all Leeann had done in the past few years to turn her life around. He'd heard enough stories about women who'd suffered like she had to know that some of them never found a way to recover.

"But finding out that someone hurt her," his mother continued in a soft voice. "That must be difficult to deal with."

Impossible. "I'm figuring it out as I go."

"Have you gotten to that punching bag yet?"

He looked at his mother in confusion. "What?"

"I was there every day when your decorators were putting your home together. Including the workout area." Val stood and went to the sink to rinse out her cup. "Perhaps you need to work out your…response to what Leeann went through, before you make any decisions. About her or the camp."

His mother was right. Talking helped, but at the moment he wanted to hit something and hit it hard. Wanted to hunt down the bastard that hurt Leeann. Wanted to roar at the injustice she'd suffered.

Val walked back to him, placing a gentle touch

to his shoulder. "Take time to make sure you want the same things Leeann does. For both your sakes."

"Well, I think that can be arranged, because I've got news for you that no one else knows about yet."

"Hmm, intriguing." His mother sat again. "What is it?"

"I'm going back to North Carolina."

Her smile disappeared. "What?"

"No, this is a good thing. I got a phone call this morning from the doctors back there. The specialist I saw yesterday in Cheyenne forwarded my test results and they want to see me right away." He grabbed her hand and gave a gentle squeeze. "They're going to evaluate my chances to get back in my race car."

"Are you going back to racing?"

"I don't know," he said, finally speaking the truth for the first time. "That was always the plan. From the moment I opened my eyes in the hospital, but now? I can't make any decisions until I know if I'm medically cleared. If I am, then I need to decide if I'm even going to try to get behind the wheel again."

His mother nodded. "I take it Dean is going with you?"

"He's getting the camper packed and ready as we speak. We're heading out tonight," Bobby said. "I don't know how long we'll be gone."

He waited, watching her closely. He could almost see the wheels turning inside her head, knowing she had something more to say.

"Please let me know how everything works out, okay? I like us being close again."

"I like it, too."

This time it was she who gave a gentle squeeze to their clasped hands. "Since you haven't asked for my opinion in all this, I'm going to keep them to myself, but if I may be allowed to say one thing?"

"Sure, go ahead."

"Does Leeann know you're leaving town?"

* * *

The knock at her front door surprised her.

Leeann pushed the mute button on the television, noting it was after nine o'clock. Dropping the remote to the sofa, she left the oversize bowl of popcorn on her seat and headed across the room.

Checking through the peephole, she was shocked to see Bobby standing in the glow from her automated porch light. She quickly undid the dead bolt and opened the door. "Hey."

He stared at her through the screen. His hair was messy, as if he'd been running his fingers through it. "Hey, yourself."

The night air was cool and she wore only her pajamas, an outfit that was nothing more than a loose-fitting tank top and a pair of hip-hugging cotton pants. She crossed her arms over her chest, a shiver running through her. "What are you doing here?"

"I'm sorry it's so late." Bobby pushed back his jacket sleeve to glance at his watch, winced, then shoved his fist into his jeans pocket. "I saw you called a couple of times."

She tried to ignore his reaction when he looked at his watch, but she automatically tucked her hair behind one ear. "I wasn't sure if we were getting together—you know, like usual, to talk about the camp. When I couldn't reach you, I thought…"

"I tried to call you back."

His statement caused a warm rush of pleasure. "Really? I had my self-defense class at the Youth Center this afternoon. Then I grabbed a shower and fell asleep. I guess I was more tired—"

"Lee, can I come inside for a minute?" Bobby cut her off, gesturing with his head over one shoulder. "I don't have long, Zip's waiting on me."

It was then she noticed the idling motor home parked by the curb. He was leaving? Bobby was leaving town?

Her finger fumbled with the screen-door latch. "Oh, of course. Come on in."

He slipped inside and closed the door behind him. Leeann backed up a few steps and bumped into her small dining-room table. The vase sitting in the center wobbled. She spun around, righting it before the beautiful blossoms spilled.

"I see you got the flowers."

Bobby's voice was low, confirming what she already knew. He still stood right by the door. She turned and before she allowed herself to second-guess the gesture, she walked back to him, laid a hand on his arm for balance and rose to her tiptoes to press a kiss to his cheek.

He tilted his head, his gaze locked with hers. "What was that for?"

She inhaled a quick breath. The cool night air clung to him, mixing with the leather of his jacket and natural woodsy scent that was all Bobby. "A thank-you. I love the flowers. They're beautiful, but I'm afraid the town's gossips are having a field day with them."

"Meaning?"

"They were delivered to me at my aunt's very crowded shop."

Bobby closed his eyes for a moment and dropped his head back. "Sorry about that. I didn't think about making sure they came directly to your place."

"It's okay." She released him and put her slippered feet back to the floor. "It seems we've been fodder for Destiny's busybodies for the last couple of weeks anyway."

"So I've learned. And that chatter's not going to go away once word gets out that I've left town."

Leeann forced what she hoped was an easy smile. "Time for a 'guys only' road trip?"

"I'm going back to North Carolina."

As silly as the saying was, Leeann was sure her heart did freeze in her chest. Still breathing, still standing, still smiling at him, but for a moment everything inside her turned to ice. She hugged her arms even closer to her and prayed her voice would be there when she opened her mouth. "So—so you're leaving now?"

Bobby nodded, his hands fisted inside his jacket pockets. "Yeah, the traffic's lighter at night."

"Well, I hope Dean's driving." When his mouth pressed into a hard line, she realized what she'd said. "Only because you look so tired. Did you get any sleep last night?"

"Some."

"I didn't mean to steal your bed."

That got her a hint of a smile. "That's okay. I wasn't anxious to get back to dreamland anyway."

An emotion flashed in his eyes. Pity? That was all she needed tonight. Turning away, she headed across the room, needing something to hold on to. "I'm sorry about that, too." She gripped the cushioned back of the sofa. "I have a feeling if I hadn't told you about my past, you would've slept easily through the night."

"The nightmare wasn't your fault."

Bobby's words fell over her bare shoulders before a cloak of warmth enveloped her. She grabbed at the bulky, patchwork quilt Bobby had taken from a nearby chair to wrap around her. "Thanks, I was a bit chilly."

"Believe me, it was more for my benefit than yours."

She faced him. "I don't understand."

"Lee, those flimsy pants you're wearing are so see-through I can read the words *KISS THIS* across your backside."

Her initial confusion quickly morphed into understanding. Heat flooded her face. "Oh! I didn't realize. I mean, if I'd known you were stopping by, I wouldn't have put them on."

He groaned low in his throat. "Damn, girl, you really are a heartbreaker."

Before she could ask him what he meant by that, Bobby held out a set of keys and a folded piece of paper. "Here, these are to my place and instructions to use the security pass code. So you can keep working on the plans while we're gone."

She palmed the items. The key ring still warm from his touch. "I wasn't dreaming. You really decided to go through with it?"

Bobby nodded, a genuine smile on his handsome face. "Yes, we're going to build a summer camp for kids."

Elation filled her and Leeann fought against doing a happy dance right then and there. She hadn't been a hundred percent sure she'd heard him correctly last night, but now Bobby was stating aloud his commitment to the project they'd worked tirelessly on for the past few weeks.

She'd hoped the enthusiasm they shared over everything from the number of needed shower stalls to a camp slogan—something they still hadn't agreed on—would help him realize this was the perfect solution for those acres of beautiful forest.

Then she remembered the reason for his visit

tonight. "But you're going back to North Carolina?"

His smile slipped a bit. "I have business obligations there that need my attention."

She'd almost forgotten how Bobby had made his fortune. Between his endorsement work and his race team, he must have many commitments down south. "How long will you be gone?"

"I don't know."

"But you're coming back, right?" She captured her bottom lip with teeth for a moment, her fists clenching the quilt close to her chest. "I mean, we still have a lot of work to do. We have a lot of things…unfinished."

"Unfinished with the camp? Yeah, you could say that." He took a couple of steps backward toward the door. "We don't even have a name for the place yet. But right now I really need to head out."

She jerked her head in a quick nod and followed him, watching as he opened the door. Gripping the handle, she swiped her tongue over her suddenly dry lips and tried to keep her words light and breezy. "Things are still unfinished between us, too, right?"

Bobby turned and stared at her for a long moment. When he reached up to caress her cheek with his fingers, she couldn't stop herself from leaning into his touch. He dipped his head ever so slightly and she was sure he was going to kiss her.

When he didn't move to close the gap between them, she forced herself to follow his lead. She settled for whispering, "Be safe."

"You, too." Then, without another word, he turned and walked away.

Chapter Thirteen

After almost two weeks that included only three quick phone calls, mostly late at night and surprisingly filled with long silences and awkward conversation, Bobby was finally heading back to Destiny today.

At least that was what his text message promised, which she'd received this morning. The problem was he was already back in town.

The only reason Leeann knew that was because she'd overheard the pretty redhead Dean had taken out a few times chatting at her aunt's hair salon that afternoon. She'd mentioned Dean calling and asking her for a date that evening.

While Leeann's cell phone remained pitifully silent.

She entered the circular drive outside Bobby's house at a quick pace, her usual smooth running form a jangled mess of nerves and unsteady breaths. Leaving her house for a run in just a windbreaker and shorts probably wasn't the smartest move now that the sun was almost gone, but her head had been so jumbled since learning of Bobby's return, she was thankful she'd remembered to put her sneakers on.

She slowed to a stop, muscles quivering from the physical exertion and the cool night air. It took a few more breaths—deep and cleansing this time—and another check of her cell phone. Nope, no calls. Reminding herself of the decision she'd come to, she found her resolve again.

Knocking on the front door, she waited. When no one came she checked the security keypad and found it turned off. Using the key Bobby had given her for only the second time, she let herself in. She'd come by once, to grab one of the laptops so she could work on the camp plans. Being here while he was away just didn't seem right.

The lights were on with the stereo tuned to the local country music station. The tasty aroma of home cooking filled the air, but the house was still. Except for the familiar growl from the canine welcoming committee at her feet.

"Hello, Daisy, nice to see you again, too." Leeann placed her hands on her hips. "Where is he?"

The dog just stared at her, but Leeann didn't flinch. "You might as well tell me. I'm not going anywhere."

Daisy turned and headed for the stairs, pausing to look back at Leeann when she didn't follow. So she joined the pup and they headed to the lower level together.

The dog offered her one last look before she disappeared into Dean's bedroom. Leeann recognized the familiar noises coming from the gym. Bobby and Dean were in the middle of a workout.

She hadn't come here to confront Bobby about the distance he'd put between them by leaving and his silence while he'd been gone. Besides, she'd figured her aunt was right, he needed time to work through everything she'd told him.

Still, the fact that he'd returned today and hadn't called her...

She squared her shoulders and took a deep breath, hoping he was ready to talk now—or at least listen—because she had plenty to say.

"You know, I've been doing a lot of thinking."

Bobby's words caused Leeann to pause just outside the door.

"No kidding?" Dean's familiar sarcastic tone made her smile. "I'd been wondering what that burning smell was—"

"Shut up and listen, okay?" Bobby cut off his friend. "I think I've come to a few decisions."

"Well, hold off on your grand announcement

for a minute. I need to get some clean towels from the laundry." Dean walked out of the exercise room, surprise lighting up his face when he spotted her standing there. "Hey—"

Leeann held her index finger to her lips, motioning for him to follow her. Amusement danced in his dark eyes, but he nodded and trailed behind her as she returned upstairs. They walked into the mudroom where the washer and dryer were located.

"Okay, you want to tell me what's going on?" Dean asked, reaching for a stack of folded towels. "And how did you know we were back in town?"

"A little redheaded birdie told me. Aren't you going to be late for your date?"

He quirked a brow at her.

"You've been back less than three hours," Leeann continued. "And you already have plans for the night."

"What can I say?" Dean grinned. "I'm good."

"And I'm going crazy. We hardly spoke the

whole time you two were gone. Something I'm sure you're aware of."

The playfulness disappeared from Dean's eyes. "He's had a lot on his mind lately."

"Bobby told you, didn't he? About my past."

A light blush crossed the man's cheeks and Leeann regretted her abrupt tone. "I'm sorry, I shouldn't have. It's okay, Dean. I never asked him to keep what happened to me just between the two of us. Even though I'm sure you've figured out it's not something I'd like shouted from the rooftops."

Dean returned her stare for a moment, then nodded, his embarrassment replaced with concern. "He needed someone to talk to. What happened to you—I know it was a long time ago and you've obviously worked through it, but it really tore him up. And you...girl, you're—"

"Amazing. Yeah, so I've been told."

"And now you're chomping at the bit to have some alone time with my buddy." Dean held out the towels toward her. "Which I totally understand. Go easy on the guy, huh? I don't think he has any idea what he's doing."

"Didn't I just hear him say he's made some sort of decision?"

"True, but he could be talking about what's for dinner."

Leeann offered him one raised eyebrow.

"Naw, I don't believe that either." Dean nodded. "Okay, I'll make myself scarce for the night."

Guilt swamped her. "You don't have to rush out right now. I mean, if you need to take a shower first."

"I'll just grab my stuff. I'm sure Katie won't mind if I get ready at her place."

Leeann rose up on tiptoe and placed a light kiss on his cheek. "You're a great guy, Dean."

"Shhh, don't let that get around." He offered her a wink while pulling out his wallet. Seconds later, he pressed a foiled packet into her hand. "Here, take this. Just in case."

"Dean!"

"Hey, a girl can't be too safe, ya know?"

A few minutes later, she saw Dean heading for the garage. Waiting until the taillights of the pickup disappeared from view, she slipped the packet into the hidden pocket of her shorts before heading back down the stairs, towels in hand.

After slowly exhaling another deep breath, she entered the gym. Bobby sat at the shoulder press machine, his back to her. With its inclined bench and overhead pulley system, it was a piece of equipment she'd seen him use often during his sessions.

Like right now.

As he raised and lowered the bar, the muscles in his shoulders and arms stretched and contracted in a smooth controlled motion, showing off miles of gleaming skin. His only clothing was dark shorts and sneakers.

"It's about time you got back." Bobby's words caused Leeann to jump as he lowered the overhead bar to its starting position with a clang. He held out one hand. "I've got a river of sweat in my eyes. Throw me a towel, would ya?"

She did as instructed, hitting him right in the head.

"Thanks." He draped the towel over his face, but kept talking. "Like I was saying, I've made a decision. I still need to talk to Leeann again about her offer to use her land and the pond for the camp, but I don't think that's going to be an issue." He quickly swiped at his face before running the towel over his chest and down each arm. "Not after I make her an offer she can't refuse."

Okay, that sounded a little Godfatherish, but darn if her heart didn't do a little flip-flop right in her chest. If that meant what she hoped it did…

"There are a couple of conditions, but I'm going to ask her to come on board as the camp's director."

Okay, that wasn't exactly what she'd wanted to hear. "Conditions?"

Bobby's head whipped around so fast he nearly fell off the bench. "Lee?"

"In the flesh."

"What the hell?" He stood. "What are you doing here?"

"Well, it's nice to see you, too." Crossing her arms over her chest, she leaned against the long table Dean used for full-body rubdowns. Ignoring the butterflies zooming around in her stomach, she prayed she looked more at ease than she felt.

The last thing she'd expected was Bobby to offer her a job. Darn her heart, she'd actually hoped for another kind of proposition all together.

"So, let's hear these conditions."

"Lee…I…" His words faltered, his gaze shot around the room. "Where's Zip?"

"He's gone. I told him I wanted to talk to you. Alone."

"You did?"

"It sounds like you want to talk to me, too. At

least long enough to make me 'an offer I can't refuse.' Wasn't that how you put it?"

"Ah, yeah, I did, but…"

When his voice trailed off, she pushed away from the table and headed across the room, but froze when Bobby took a step backward. He bumped into the machine and landed hard on his butt, straddling the bench again.

He didn't want her close to him?

The question caused an explosion of pain to envelop her body, clouding her already mangled thoughts. She stared at him, but he wouldn't even hold her gaze.

"Lee, I'm in the middle of workout." He looked straight ahead, his gaze on the archway that led to the pool. "I don't think this is the time or place—"

"I think this is the perfect time and place." She cut his words off, moving forward until she stood in front of him. "What's the problem? I'm dressed for a workout. I'll join you."

His eyes snapped to hers, wide and unblinking. "You'll what?"

"Will that make it easier for you? Because what we really need to discuss isn't the camp, it's us. I get that you needed time to deal with...to come to terms with my past. Which I'd hoped you might have thought about once or twice while you were out of town."

Bobby fell back against the incline, one hand held out as if to stop her. "Lee, wait—"

"No, I'm not going to wait. Not one moment longer. Forgive me, but I'm assuming you used some of that time away to come to a conclusion about me, about us."

"I did. I have." He moved his hand to the overhead bar and gripped it tight. "Dammit, you heard me say I want you working—"

"I'm not talking about the camp! I'm talking about me wanting you in my life, wanting you in every way a woman wants a man."

She looked up, and her frustration dissolved into a longing she'd never felt before as she caught Bobby watching her. His gaze blazed hot as it started at her feet and slowly traveled up her legs. He paused for a moment at where her hand rested between her breasts.

Her determination weakened as uncertainty crept in, but she pushed onward, pulling down the zipper until it stopped just above her belly button. "And I don't mean that I need you as a way to fix the past or make me whole again, because I am whole."

That got his attention back to her face. She took another step forward until her leg brushed against his, his skin cool and damp. "I'm a woman who made a decision about what she wants and needs. That's you, but if you don't—"

"I do."

The certainty in his voice, in his eyes, suddenly had her hopes soaring in a way that just moments ago didn't seem possible. This rollercoaster ride of emotions was making her dizzy.

"You do what exactly?"

That sexy, roguish smile returned. "Want you, too."

She opened her mouth, but for the first time tonight, she didn't know what to say. Snapping her mouth shut, she caught her bottom lip between her teeth just to make sure she didn't say the wrong thing.

"Look what you do to me," she finally said, unable to remain quiet. "You get me so crazy, I can't—I don't think before I speak or come barging into your home."

"Lee, the distance between us, both figuratively and literally, isn't because I don't want to be with you." He dropped his hands to his lap, the towel fisted in his grip. "Yes, I had to deal with my anger over what happened to you, but I thought it was pretty clear that night in my bed how much I desired you. You're the one who had to be sure of what you wanted, for whatever reasons."

"Whatever reasons? What does that mean?"

His naked chest expanded as he inhaled a deep

breath, then released it. He dropped the towel and reached for her hand, gently tugging it from where she'd grabbed on to her windbreaker. "It means that however you want me, for however long you want me, I'm here."

Just like that, almost twenty years after they'd met, Leeann Harris fell in love with Bobby Winslow all over again.

She returned his gentle squeeze then used his hand for balance as she easily straddled him, loving the surprise that came over his features at her spontaneous move.

"What—what are you doing?"

His question sounded more like a strangled plea. Leeann released his hand, placing hers on his wide shoulders. The hairs on his legs tickled as she slowly slid closer to his chest.

A hot blush crept over her skin as she encountered the physical evidence that he was as aroused as she.

Keeping her gaze locked with his, she watched Bobby's expression morph from surprise to desire. Her fingertips pressed into his muscles, his strength an anchor she could hold on to, relax into, as she reassured herself who she was with and what she was doing.

Making love. Her and Bobby.

Without thought, she pushed up on her toes, her hips pressing against his, cradling his erection between her thighs. "Is this okay?"

He raised his hands to the overhead bar, his grip causing the muscles in his arms, chest and washboard abs to tighten, flex and ripple. "This is perfect, Lee. As long as you're sure?"

"I've never been surer of anything in my life." She leaned forward then pressed her mouth to his.

The kiss was tender and sweet, despite their position and state of undress. He sipped at her as she brushed her mouth back and forth over his. He tasted salty and minty and she eagerly parted her lips, urging him onward as the kiss deepened and lengthened.

Her windbreaker—too warm, too confining—

stuck to her skin. She briefly released Bobby from their kiss to yank it over her head. The need to be skin on skin had her pulling her arms free.

When his eyes glazed over, she was glad she'd kept on the baby-blue lace bra instead of trading for the sporty style.

Wanting to remember this moment, she concentrated on taking it all in. The bright lights, the tangy smell of chlorinated water, the soft country music in the background. She stamped onto her memory the strength of his powerful legs beneath her backside, the sheen of his damp skin and the potent longing in his eyes.

For her.

Letting her jacket fall to the floor behind her, she dragged one bra strap, then the other, from her shoulders. They hung loose against her arms, the lace clinging to her breasts. She dropped her hands to Bobby's chest. His heartbeat thumped strong against her fingertips as she brushed her lips over his again.

Bobby reared up, capturing her mouth. She pressed even closer, their hips moving in a natural rhythm. The friction of their clothes heightened her anticipation.

It was then Leeann realized he still held tight to the metal bar over their heads.

She broke free and straightened, closing her eyes against the sudden sting of her tears. Blindly, she trailed her fingers over the corded muscles of his arm until she reached his wrists, then his clenched fists.

"Lee, I don't want to hurt—to scare—"

His voice was as rough as his touch was gentle when she pried his fingers loose. She let her head fall back, opening herself to him, then placed one hand to her breast.

"Touch me, Bobby, please."

His fingers brushed over her skin; soon one hand became two. Still she kept her head back, eyes closed. His hands went to the tiny front clasp of her bra and with a simple twist it opened and disappeared from her body.

He shifted, rising, bringing their bodies together as he wrapped one arm around her waist, his mouth now at her neck.

"It's me, it's Bobby," he whispered against her skin.

Leeann brought her head forward, her hands sliding into his damp wavy hair. "I know."

"You are so beautiful, Lee."

He cupped her breast, taking her taut nipple into the wet heat of his mouth. Gentle suctions, the rasp of his tongue, created sensations that had her flying. She rocked her hips as he moved from one breast to the other, his mouth never leaving her skin.

"Bobby, please…" She dropped one hand between her thighs, stroking the length of him through the cotton material of his shorts, loving how he responded with low, guttural groans.

"Let's—" His mouth moved up her neck again until he reached her ear. "Let's go upstairs."

She shook her head. Everything was perfect right here. She wanted the bright lights, wanted to see his face as he made love to her, wanted to be the one in control this first time.

How could she tell him all that? How could she explain without breaking the magical spell they'd woven around each other in these past moments? "No, please...I want to be with you right here, right now."

His hands moved to her waist and gave a gentle squeeze. He understood. Without words, without details, he knew exactly what she needed and why.

He leaned back, a slight grin on his sexy face. "I don't have anything—any protection here."

She braced her hands on his rock-hard thighs and slowly pushed herself off his lap. Never taking her eyes from his, she toed off her sneakers and then her socks before pulling the tiny foil packet from the pocket of her shorts.

His smile widened. "You planned this?"

"Let's just say I had high hopes."

She tossed him the packet, then tucked her thumbs into the edge of her shorts and slowly pushed them and the matching blue-lace panties down over her hips.

Bobby mirrored her actions, removing his shorts. She helped by sliding off his sneakers. He quickly sheathed himself. As if he couldn't stand them being apart for one more minute, he pulled her back onto his lap, his mouth taking hers in a heated kiss.

She held on to his shoulders as she again pushed herself to her toes, sliding over him. His hands were at her waist, supporting her, guiding her.

"Slow and easy, honey," Bobby whispered against her mouth. "Take all the time you need."

Her eyes locked with his. She allowed him to see deep inside her heart as she took him deep inside her body. He filled her completely and she slowly moved, becoming reacquainted with his fullness.

Her hands moved to his jaw, cradling his face as he pulled her close, aligning his cheek to hers. His uneven, desire-filled words of encouragement, almost incoherent at times, created a delicious heat inside her that grew and built.

She felt his controlled restraint and it pushed her higher, knowing he was holding back for her. She loved him all the more for it.

"That's it, baby, right there. Slow and easy. Yes…"

A tiny moan caught in her throat as her body swelled and convulsed. Shuddering sensations caused her to tighten around him. He let her know how close he was; she was right there with him. Together they fell over the edge.

Moments passed as they clung to each other, their breathing a seesaw action until they found a slow, matching rhythm.

"Please tell me I can take you to my bed." Bobby's words were a reverent whisper. "Tell me this night isn't over. I've finally got you in my arms again. I'm not letting go."

His words thrilled her as she pressed kisses to his forehead, closed eyelids, the tip of his nose. "I'm not going anywhere but upstairs with you."

She finished with a hard press to his mouth. "As soon as I can find the strength to move."

"Hold on to me."

Forever, she thought, *forever and ever.*

Chapter Fourteen

A half hour must've passed before Bobby had tried to stand with Leeann in his arms, but she'd spouted off so many reasons for him not to play the hero and try to sweep her off her feet, he finally shut her up with a deep kiss.

Then they'd grabbed a couple of robes from the pool area, gathered their scattered clothes and walked to his room instead, arm in arm, whispering and laughing, touching.

She'd stiffened when they entered his dark bedroom, so he'd quickly hit the light switch that turned on the lamps on either side of his bed. Then he'd headed for the bathroom declaring he needed a shower, his heart flipping over when she shyly asked if he wanted company. They'd enjoyed his glass-enclosed, multihead shower and amidst the bright lights and pounding spray, he made love to her all over again.

After they finally crawled beneath the sheets, he'd reached for the light, but Lee's hesitant touch stopped him. It tore at him when she said she never slept in complete darkness. He reminded her of that night in his bed a couple of weeks ago, but she pointed out his television had been on.

The lights stayed on. Not that their brightness stopped them from drifting off to sleep.

It was almost midnight when Bobby awoke, loving the feel of Leeann in his arms as she lay sprawled across his chest.

"Hmm, I'm starving," she mumbled, snuggling into him. "What's that wonderful smell?"

Bobby looked down at her, still not quite believing what had happened between them in the past few hours. He'd never expected her to show up tonight, despite the overwhelming need to call her once he and Zip crossed the state line.

Hell, he'd wanted to talk to her every day he was gone, but he'd been crazy busy for hours at a time with all the things he needed to take care of before heading back to Wyoming.

Things he now needed to talk about with her.

Her eyelids fluttered open and she tilted her head back to look at him. Golden hazel eyes, soft and sleepy. Bobby's heart pounded out an erratic beat as he read the naked emotion on her face.

She loved him.

And he loved her.

Neither of them had said the words aloud, so maybe he was making assumptions, but he knew that his heart had always belonged to this lady, even during their years apart. But was love going to be enough?

"Bobby?"

What had she asked him? Oh, right. "Ah, that's a Crock-Pot of spicy Italian chicken that's been slow-cooking for most of the day."

"You haven't even been back in Destiny that long."

He smiled at her. "Zip made it in the camper's kitchen in the early hours of this morning somewhere between Lincoln, Nebraska, and here."

"Well, it smells amazing." The rumbling of her stomach had both of them laughing. Leeann sat up, holding the sheet to her breasts. "And since I'm obviously running close to empty, I'm going to make up a tray and bring it back here. You hungry?"

He reached out to brush his thumb over her full bottom lip, his gaze traveling over her beautiful neck, bare shoulders and toned arms. "Yeah, you could say that."

"I meant for food, cowboy. Man—or woman for that matter—cannot live on love alone."

Her words caused both of them to go still. Then Leeann dropped the sheet and crawled out of the bed. The sight of her gorgeous nakedness took his breath away, even after she covered it with one of the robes from the end of the bed.

"So, do I bring back enough for two?"

Bobby hated that she wasn't looking at him, but he didn't know what to say other than, "Sure. I'm starving, too."

She padded out of the room.

He headed for the bathroom, grabbing a pair of sweats from his dresser on the way. Returning, he straightened the covers, propped up the pillows and sat again. He stretched out his legs, crossed his ankles then uncrossed them. The remote control for the television sat next to the bed, but he resisted the temptation.

In its place, he grabbed the remote for the gas fireplace and seconds later, a fiery blaze warmed the room. Pressing another button, he dimmed the lights now that the fire added a glow to the room.

Setting the scene for more romance instead of talking?

A flash of guilt stole over him.

He and Leeann needed to talk. About the camp, about what happened during his time back in North Carolina, about the future. But did it have to happen tonight?

Weren't they allowed a bit more time away from the craziness of the outside world? They were finally connected again. He didn't want to jeopardize that.

Leeann came back into the room, a large tray in her hands teeming with dishes of steaming food, a bottle of wine, glasses and napkins.

"This stuff is amazing," she said, smiling as she set the tray in the middle of the bed. "I couldn't resist tasting it as I pulled everything together."

Bobby grabbed the wine and glasses and moved them to the bedside table. He poured as Leeann hiked her robe to midthigh and gingerly joined him, being careful not to upset the food. The deep neckline of the robe gaped open and he could see the creamy curve of her breasts.

She handed him a plate filled with slices of Italian bread and spicy chicken then took the wineglass he offered her. As she leaned back to place it on the table next to her, the material covering her legs silently slid to the side, revealing her long legs.

Suddenly food was the last thing on his mind.

After she lifted her own plate, he noticed the laptop nestled at the bottom of the tray.

"I know, I know." She waved at the computer and the robe's opening separated another inch. "What can I say? It called to me and I was helpless to resist."

He was starting to know the feeling.

"I didn't realize computers could do that sort of thing," he said, forking a pile of chicken onto the bread before taking a huge bite.

She grinned and did the same, a look of ecstasy rushing over her features as she chewed.

Okay, that helpless feeling of surrender just centered itself in Bobby's lap.

"Oh, my, this is good," she moaned around

a mouthful of food. "I've got to get the recipe from Dean."

"Forget it. He guards it like a state secret," Bobby said with a grin, loving this side of her as he took another mouthful of food and chewed. "It's the one meal he can make that the ladies can't say no to."

"I can understand why. It's the best thing in the world."

He sank into the comforter, lowering to one elbow and bringing their bodies closer together. He trailed his fingers high on her thigh, slowly gathering the cotton material of her robe until he found her smooth, warm skin. "Hmm, I wouldn't say it's the best thing."

She leaned toward him, her hair falling slowly to curtain her face. Her lips parted in a silent request. He complied, letting her set the pace as her mouth settled on his. Lightly teasing, then more urgent and pressing, she explored his mouth. He loved her taste, one part spicy and one part sweet. A mix of chicken, wine and her, it was a heady combination that left him wanting more, wanting her all over again.

Ending the kiss with a low growl of approval, Bobby took her almost empty plate, laid it atop his, then set them next to the wine. He got rid of the tray and turned back to her.

She slowly pulled one end of the robe's belt until it loosened and gave way.

Her chin lifted in that familiar proud tilt as she parted the material, revealing herself to his heated gaze. He quickly rid himself of his sweat-pants, crawled back across the bed and moved between her open legs.

Gently pinning her to the bed beneath him, he heard her rush of breath as she clung to his arms. He loved the feel of her spread beneath him, but he held back his desperate longing to press their bodies together.

"Is this okay?" he whispered, supporting his weight on his forearms as he traced her cheek with his finger. "The first two times you were… well, the one in control."

"Considering we were standing in your shower the last time I think that was more fifty-fifty." She shifted her hips, pressing the hot ridge of his erection to her belly. "And this is definitely okay."

"One word…" He slipped his finger to her chin and made her look at him. "That's all you need to say."

"I know," she whispered. "I know."

He buried his face against her neck, touching a trail to her breasts with his hands. Molding, shaping, his mouth followed the same path. The need to touch her, to mark her with his kisses over every inch of her body, played havoc with his control.

Perfection, he wanted nothing but perfection for her. Caressing, stroking, he moved across her body, moved lower until he kissed the flatness of her belly as one finger, then two, dipped even lower and slipped inside her wet heat. Soon his kisses were there, too.

"Bobby."

His name burst from her lips as she arched against his mouth, offering herself completely, taking all he gave her. He ignored his body's aching need for release, spurred on by the shivering sensations that told him she was close, so close.

"Now, please..." She tugged on his arms. "Want you now..."

He rose over her and paused to protect them both before lifting her hips. She entwined one leg with his, the other clasped around his waist as he entered her.

"Forever, Lee," he whispered against her lips. "This is forever."

Not wanting to rush, he tried to hold back, but her tremors pulled him in, giving him the love, hope and peace he could only find deep inside this woman.

He cried out her name as his passion joined hers, the two of them clinging to each other as they spiraled out of control.

She pulled him close as their breathing slowed,

her mouth seeking his. Returning her soft kisses, he brushed her hair from her face and found tears on her cheeks.

"Ah, damn, Lee..." He started to back away.

"No, don't go." She tightened her grip with her arms and legs and held on with a fierceness that surprised him. "Please, don't go."

"I won't," he promised. "I'm right here."

Rolling to one side, he took her with him, still clad in her robe, her body locked with his, until he lay on his back. He held her close as she tucked her head onto his shoulder, her continued tears soaking his skin.

"Happy...they're happy tears," she whispered against his collarbone. "I was scared that part of me was gone forever. Thank you, thank you for giving me back...me."

Bobby tightened his hold and closed his eyes, ignoring the sting and trail of wetness that ran down into his hairline.

He didn't know how long they stayed like that,

but he was unwilling to move even after he felt her muscles give way and relax with sleep.

Watching the reflection of the fire dance against the wooden beams of the ceiling, Bobby thought back to the few afternoons he'd spent with a therapist and the books he'd devoured in the past ten days in an attempt to educate himself on what she'd gone through.

It'd take time, but he'd been determined to let go of his anger and concentrate on the here and now. She'd come so far in accepting her life and how it had turned out, he didn't want to set her back.

The future.

They had to look to the future.

Hours passed until dawn arrived, the rising sun breaking through the trees. He finally left her in the bed, covering her with blankets as she continued to sleep.

Pulling on his sweats, he took their plates to the kitchen and started a pot of coffee before checking on Daisy, guessing correctly that Zip hadn't made it home last night. The pup eagerly pawed at the glass doors in Zip's room that led to the patio. Bobby let her out and then fed her when she followed him back to the kitchen.

After washing the dishes, he grabbed one large glass of orange juice for Lee and a coffee for himself and returned to his bedroom, knowing they needed to talk about their future.

Leeann turned when Bobby entered the room, loving the sight of him in nothing but sweatpants that rode low on his hips. Making love with him was everything she'd dreamed it would be, and more. He was home again, and after last night all her doubts had disappeared.

She read the surprise on his face at finding her awake and sitting up in bed. "I woke up a few minutes ago and you were gone."

"Daisy had to go out."

He handed her a tall glass of juice and she drank deeply, then she reached for the laptop lying next to her on the bed, already up and running. "Thanks, I needed that. I thought we could start the day with me bringing you up-to-date on what I've come up with for the camp while you were gone."

"How do you wake up so fast?" He took a long slug from his mug. "And without any caffeine."

"It's a gift." She watched him walk around the end of the bed, enjoying the view of his wide shoulders and six-pack abs even as a different kind of passion pumped through her veins at the moment. "So, the camp layout is pretty much complete, meaning sections of the land could be cleared this year. Next summer should be a lot of fun as we watch the buildings go up."

She crossed her legs, tucking in the robe around her, her excitement growing as she shared her thoughts.

"I think the Murphys are going to have to hire an extra crew just for this job, which will be good news for the area. Depending on how far they get, maybe we could do a trial run by the summer's end? Use just local kids to work out the kinks?"

"Lee, wait a minute."

"I know, I know, I'm a ball of energy." Her fingers pounded on the keyboard as she literally bounced against the pillows. She grinned, looking up at him. "A surprise maybe, considering our night together, but never underestimate the power of a nap."

"I won't. Jeez, I'm getting tired just watching you."

She pulled in a deep breath. "So, I was wondering what your title is going to be if I get Camp Director. Let me guess, something fancy like Chief Executive Officer?"

Bobby stared down into his coffee mug. "More along the lines of Daddy Warbucks."

"Ah, yes, you're the money behind this venture, but I want to contribute, too. I don't have much left in savings, unless we consider that my paycheck until…" Leeann's voice trailed off as she realized he wasn't really engaged in the conversation. "Bobby, what is it?"

He walked to the dresser and set the mug down. "Lee, we need to talk."

"Isn't that what we've been doing?" A shiver of unease made her set aside the computer and join him as she stared out the large window at the forest. "I don't understand. You don't seem as excited—oh, no, you're not going to be involved."

"Of course, I'm involved." Frowning, he turned to her. "It's my land."

"I'm talking about the day-to-day operations, being there every day as each building goes up." She took a step away from him. "Being there when we're deciding on mattresses and dinnerware, when we're finally filled up with kids swimming, hiking, playing softball, whatever we come up with. Wait, is this one of those conditions you mentioned last night?"

Bobby reached for her before she had a chance to move farther away. "One of the conditions is that I don't want to just hire you as an employee. I want you be a part owner."

"Owner? With you?"

"Yes."

"So that means you're going to be here, in Destiny?"

Giving her hands a gentle squeeze, he pulled her toward the matching set of chairs near the window. "Please, sit. I need to tell you something—"

A rumbling noise, faint at first then growing louder, cut off his words.

"What on earth is that?" Leeann asked, turning toward the sound. "It sounds like it's coming from your driveway."

"Because it is," Bobby groaned. "That would be my crew chief and some of my team in an oversize pickup hauling a trailer. With my car inside."

"Your car? Meaning your race car?" Confusion swamped her. "I thought the accident destroyed..."

"That was a test car, Lee. Listen, I went back to North Carolina because part of my business obligations with my race team included a follow-up appointment with my doctors. They needed to evaluate whether I can drive again."

"You are driving."

"I mean professionally."

"Doctors…" Puzzlement filled her, until the words sunk in and she realized what he was saying. Her knees buckled and she sank into the chair. "You never said anything the few times we talked."

He dropped into a crouch next to her. "I know. I should have, but there was so much going on. Meeting with the lawyers to get financials for the camp set up, reviewing endorsement contracts with my agents and yes, doctor appointments. They put me through a series of rigorous tests for three days in a row."

She remembered how exhausted he sounded one night when she'd finally got him on the phone. He'd practically fallen asleep while they tried to talk. The fact he'd never mentioned anything about the testing caused a raw spot of pain to form in her chest.

"You're returning to racing? The doctors cleared you?"

"I've been cleared to do some test runs. The final decision of my return to the circuit is mine."

"So why is your race car here?"

"I don't want a media circus, despite my agent insisting this was a big event." Bobby sighed. "I figured by bringing my car here I could do some runs out at Miller's Point before I made any firm decisions about the next step."

Leeann stood. "That old dirt track outside of town? That's just a place where locals drag race."

"It's where I started racing, back in high school." Bobby stood as well. "Zip and I have been out there a few times. It's still in good condition and well maintained. If I can handle the car, the speeds out there, then a regulation track will be a breeze."

"And if you crash again?" Her palms moistened as a wave of fear went over her. She didn't

WELCOME HOME, BOBBY WINSLOW

think she could live through that experience again. Seeing his crash on TV had about done her in. How much worse would witnessing it in person be? She didn't think she'd survive if something happened to him.

Silence filled the air until a loud knocking at the front door caused both of them to jump.

"Lee, don't leave. Not like this."

"Like what?" She spun to face him. "You've obviously got this all figured out. I guess I really screwed up your plans by showing up last night, huh?"

He advanced on her. "You didn't screw up anything. Last night was the best night of my life."

She looked down at her clothes clutched in her fists. Last night was the start of a new life for her, for them. At least she'd thought so. "Mine, too."

"But racing is what I am, it's what I do." Bobby spoke softly, but with purpose. "I have to know if I still have it in me to compete, to be a winner."

She heard the fervor in his voice and at the same moment she envied his confidence in who he was and what he wanted. "All this time, ever since New York, I've been searching for that same direction and purpose in my own life. I already love the camp and it's nothing but a pile of paperwork and bunch of trees."

The knocking came again, more insistent this time, cutting her off. Leeann backed away, moving toward the bathroom. "You have to go. They're waiting for you."

Bobby nodded, grabbing a T-shirt and his sneakers. "I'll get them settled and then we'll talk some more."

What more could they say to each other? She couldn't ask him to walk away from something that was such a part of him, but the fear of losing him all over again was too much to bear. And not just to the dangers of his career, but the physical distance between them—her here in Destiny with the camp, him traveling nine months out of the year with his race team. How could a relationship survive that?

Willing back the tears, Leeann pulled on her clothes and ran her fingers through her hair. She left his bedroom and paused in front of a hall window, staring as he greeted his team.

The group of them walked to the end of the trailer and seconds later, his race car slowly appeared, being pushed by a couple of his crew.

She slipped out to the front porch, hidden from view by the stacked rock column, watching as Bobby walked around the front end of the vehicle, one hand lovingly caressing the smooth hood.

"It's good to see her again, huh?"

Bobby smiled at his crew member. "Yeah, real good."

That smile, so easy and natural, had Leeann brushing away tears, taking a deep breath and straightening her shoulders.

She could do this. Walk right by them and make it home before she let go of the plans she'd created inside her head, her heart, over the past week for the two of them.

Plans she'd thought had come to fruition after Bobby's whispered words of forever.

What was that saying? Life happens while you're busy making other plans?

Forcing her feet down the steps, she moved at a quick pace past the trailer, the car, the men and Bobby.

"Lee, wait. I'll drive you home."

She offered a quick wave and even managed a smile in his direction as she glanced over her shoulder. "That's okay. I need the exercise. Talk to you l-later."

Picking up speed, she managed to run the length of his driveway and disappear around the first corner before the tears reappeared.

Chapter Fifteen

The tears wouldn't stop. No matter how often Leeann brushed them from her eyes, pinched the bridge of her nose or sopped them up with the wad of tissues she'd grabbed from Bobby's bathroom. Nothing worked.

Despite her self-control during the few minutes she'd stood outside his house, the waterworks had started the moment she'd walked out of Bobby's bathroom and saw his bed, the laptop…that darn juice glass.

Unlike the mild tears from the glorious way

he'd made love to her that last time, these were hot, gut-wrenching sobs dredged from depths she hadn't even known existed, making it almost impossible to see.

She'd never cried like this before. Not after the attack, not over the loss of her parents, not even while in therapy where she had released her anger and anguish in ways that led to her defensive training and daily runs.

She ran through the center of town, taking the shortest route to her place, grateful it was still so early that few people were out yet.

The idea of going back to her empty house caused her stomach to tighten even further. She could go to Ursula, but her aunt had never been a morning person.

Then she noticed Gage walking across the parking lot toward the sheriff's office. Would Racy be up and moving yet? She hated the idea of waking her friend, but she desperately needed someone to talk to.

Grabbing her cell phone, she hit the button for the Steele family home and waited.

Four rings later, and then, "Hello?"

"Hi, Racy, it's me. Did I wake you?" She hoped the catch in her breath wasn't as obvious to Racy as it sounded to her.

"Hey, Leeann. No, you didn't wake me. Unfortunately, the little buggers doing somersaults inside me are early risers, just like their father."

Racy's pregnancy glow even carried through the airwaves. Why did that just make the tears flow harder?

"Are you all right? You don't sound too good," Racy continued. "Are you out running? What's going on?"

The tears slowed as Leeann turned down her street. She tried to take a deep breath, but that only caused a coughing fit that forced her to walk instead.

It took a few minutes before she could finally speak. "Like most things in my life, it's long and complicated. If I bring you a box of doughnut holes, can I come over?"

"Sure, but forget the food. I've been craving blueberries lately and I've got fresh muffins about to come out of the oven. I'll put on a pot of tea, too. How long before you get here?"

"I'm almost home. Let me shower first. A half hour too soon?"

"The door will be unlocked, just come on in."

Leeann actually made it out to Racy and Gage's log home on the edge of Echo Lake in twenty minutes. The house wasn't on the scale of Bobby's mansion, but with three bedrooms it was warm and inviting.

Her friend met her at the front door with a prolonged hug and no questions, which of course, started the tears all over again.

"Give me a minute alone, okay?"

"You sure?" Racy asked.

Leeann nodded and headed for the nearby half bath, Racy telling her to take all the time she needed and to join her at the dining-room table when she was ready.

It took a few more minutes to turn off the waterworks. Splashing cool water on her face helped. Leeann exited the bath, bringing the box of tissues with her just in case. When she reached the table, she sank into the closest chair. Racy slid a steaming mug of tea under her nose. Leeann gratefully wrapped her hands around the warmth and took a sip.

"That jerk better have a good reason for making you cry or I'm going to rip out his heart with a spoon."

Leeann sputtered around the rim of the mug. "Racy!"

"This is all Bobby's fault, right?"

Shaking her head, Leeann returned the mug to the table. "Actually, it's my fault."

"I don't believe that." Racy tossed her red hair over one shoulder. "But go ahead and spill."

Through two cups of tea, three muffins and a half box of tissues, Leeann told her friend everything, ending with her running away from Bobby's place that morning.

Racy gave her hand a gentle squeeze. "You're in love with the guy."

"That's it? That's all you have?" Leeann rose and went to the stove, pouring herself another mug of hot water. "Of course I'm in love with him. I knew that before I went to his house last night."

She turned back to find her friend smiling at her.

"So, what do you need from me?" Racy asked.

"Tell me how you deal with Gage's job." Leeann rejoined her friend. "I worked in law enforcement for three years, but I never thought about it from a loved one's point of view."

"Well, Destiny isn't a hotbed of criminal activity, but that didn't stop Gage from getting shot," Racy said. "By my own brother, no less."

"I remember you in the hospital. You were so scared."

Racy nodded, her eyes taking on a faraway

look. "Mainly because Gage had no idea how much I loved him and wanted him in my life."

"But now you two are married with babies on the way. You must worry about him."

"Every day, but I trust in his training, his experience and the other members of the sheriff's department to have his back." She blinked and focused again on Leeann. "Loving someone means loving all of them, the good and the not so good, especially if that happens to be their job. Being sheriff is who Gage is, it's as much a part of him as his family or his black-and-white view of the world. If Bobby chooses to continue his career in racing, you need to either support that or..."

"Or not be with him." Leeann finished Racy's sentence, then propped her elbows on the table, resting her chin in her hands. "Okay, so the dangers of his profession aside, I thought...I hoped the camp was something we would do together, but even with his new home and his family here, his racing business is still down in Carolina."

"That's true. But rumor has it Bobby originally planned to bring his business to Destiny, to build the facilities he needed on his land." Racy picked up another muffin, broke off a piece and popped it in her mouth. "Land he's since decided to use for something that has awakened a sense of purpose in you."

Leeann nodded, fresh tears welling at the corners of her eyes.

"So you're telling me he's deliberately building something he knows is going to keep us apart?"

"No, what I am saying is maybe he's creating the camp as a way to keep Destiny, and you, as his home no matter where he is. I think that says a lot about how much he loves you. The question is what are you going to do about it?"

Damn, for being a secret there were a lot of people here.

Bobby glanced at the crowd gathered along the chain-link fence that separated the dirt track from the spectator area. Not even nine in the morning yet, and there had to be at least fifty people standing around. Including his mother, who stood farther away in the stands along with Racy, Maggie and Landon.

The law was here, too. Gage had already explained to Bobby and his crew that if the track's owner allowed people in, there was nothing he could do about it.

"So much for keeping your first time back behind the wheel quiet, huh?" Zip joined Bobby where he stood next to his car.

"I guess a few digital pictures and a home video showing up on the internet won't be too bad." Bobby tugged on the flap collar of his racing suit, not used to the tight fit. "Unless, of courses, I give as good a show as the last time."

"You sure you're up for this?"

He appreciated the concern in his buddy's voice. "Yeah, it's time."

"So, can I wave the checkered flag?"

Bobby laughed. "There are no flags on a test run. What are you, twelve?"

"Aw, come on." Zip offered his best grin. "I'll do the green to start you off and black-and-white to finish."

"Fine. Whatever."

He scanned the crowd, but came up empty. Again. He couldn't help it. He hadn't been able to stop looking ever since they arrived an hour ago.

"I haven't seen her either," Zip said. "Did you try calling this morning?"

"No, I left a couple of voice mails last night. She never called me back." Bobby yanked on his helmet and adjusted the chinstrap. "Right now I need to concentrate on nothing but dropping the hammer."

"Good luck, buddy." Zip held out his hand.

"Thanks, Zip." Bobby returned his handshake, squeezing tight for a moment longer. "Without you, I wouldn't be here. You know that, don't you?"

"Don't get mushy on me now, big guy. Next

thing I know you'll be trying to hire me for that pint-size, backwoods adventure park of yours."

Bobby grinned. "It's going to need a medical staff."

"A physical therapist?"

"You could go back to med school."

A shadow passed over Zip's eyes, then his trademark grin returned. "Let's figure out one career at a time, huh? This is your turn to be making decisions."

Bobby nodded. Yes, it was, and after a few turns around this track, he'd have his answer. He'd devoted ten years of his life to racing and had enjoyed more successes than most, both on and off the track. Was it enough?

"You ready, boss?"

Turning to his crew chief, Bobby listened as he reviewed the slight modifications they'd done for alignment and balance. From the corner of his eye, he saw Zip jog halfway down the long stretch of straight track, two rolled flags in his hands.

"Give your radio headset a test."

Bobby did as instructed, ensuring he and his crew could hear each other just fine. He then got into his car. With his chief's help, he secured the racing harness. One final handshake, a tradition since they'd started working together, and his chief hung the window net.

Then it was only Bobby and his machine.

When he hit the ignition switch, number twenty-seven came alive. He ran his hand over the steering wheel, said a quick prayer then put the car into gear.

"Okay, boss, take it slow and easy for the first couple of laps." The voice came through his earpiece. "Let us know when you plan to push it."

"Roger that."

The first lap was no faster than what he put his T-bird through on the back roads of Destiny. Bobby waited for the inevitable flashbacks from his accident to appear, but they didn't. Second time around he picked up speed, enjoying the feel of the car beneath him, around him.

It felt good, familiar.

"Okay, I think I'm going to open it up," Bobby said. "Tell Zip to get ready with the green."

"Boss, you got—oh, hell, hold on a minute."

A crackling noise filled Bobby's ears. What the heck was going on? Was there a problem with the headset? Or did his crew pick up something wrong with the car?

"Bobby?"

The sweetest voice he'd ever heard came over the air. His heart pounded, threatening to burst from his chest.

"Bobby...it's me, Leeann."

His grip tightened on the wheel. "Yeah, I know who this is."

"I...um, I wanted to talk...to you before you started."

He heard the hesitation in her voice, but had no idea what it meant. "Talk now. I'm a captive audience."

"Oh, this is harder than I thought it would be."

She was dumping him. No matter the outcome

of today's run, she was walking away. It'd been fun, catching up with an old love, but sorry, she wasn't interested anymore. In the camp or him.

"Just spit it out, Lee," he growled. "Be your usual direct self."

"I love you."

His hands jerked. The back end of his car fish-tailed as he rounded the curve. Letting off the gas, he slowed, righting his position.

"Bobby! Are you okay?"

Yeah, he was just dandy. Jeez, he'd never expected her to say that. "I'm fine. Tell them I'm fine."

She relayed his message to whoever stood nearby. He slowed the car as he drove the long straightway opposite of the crowd. Opposite of where Leeann was standing right now.

"Say it again," he demanded. "I want to make sure I heard you correctly."

"I love you and I want us to be together. Forever."

As long as you quit racing.

He waited for the ultimatum, but it never came.

"Maybe this should wait," she continued. "I don't want to distract you—"

"You're not," he insisted. "Keep talking."

"Bobby—"

"Lee, I've been driving a race car for the last ten years. I have it under control." He cut off her protest. There was no way he was going to let her stop now. "You obviously thought what you had to say was important enough to get on the headset. So keep talking."

"No matter what you do, or where we end up, as long as we're together and you love me as much as I love you, we'll be happy." Leeann's words were soft yet they held an underlying strength and purpose. "The last few years have taught me that I'm in control of the good things in my life and I can handle the bad. The last few weeks showed me that I don't want to face one more day without the best thing in my life. That's you."

Stunned, he didn't know what to say.

"Your crew chief is insisting I hand the headset back to him—"

"Lee, wait."

"I'll be at the finish line. Please drive carefully."

The crackling noise was back and Bobby knew the next voice would be—

"So, are we going for it on this next lap?" His chief's deep growl filled his ear. "Or should we call it a day so I can pop open a cold one?"

What he really wanted was to get Leeann back on the line but he had to take care of business first. "It's too early for a beer, chief. Let's do this."

He came around the last turn. Zip waved the green flag furiously and Bobby pushed the gas pedal deeper into the floor. Soon the world outside was a blur except for the hard-packed dirt in front of him. This was his world, this was what he did best and it felt so good to be back here. In control, pushing the limits, watching the tachometer climb as his confidence did the same.

He was back.

Bobby Winslow, racing champion, had survived a crash that almost took his life and could've ended his career.

Damn straight, he was back.

Nothing else compared to what he was doing right at this moment…except the woman he loved with all his heart.

Leeann was his world now; she held his heart, mind and soul as surely as if she rode shotgun right next to him, just like she used to.

He wanted her, every day, every night. He wanted a pack of kids roaming that big house. He wanted to get her a dog that would sleep at the end of their bed.

He wanted to create a world where kids could just be kids, without worrying about cliques, money or what they were going to do during the long summer months except sitting in front of the television or playing on a computer.

He wanted all of that more than he wanted this. And that easily, he made his decision.

"You're looking good, boss. Top speed, smooth ride. Ready to bring it in?"

Yeah, he was ready. "Tell my buddy to wave the checkered flag. This ride is done."

One final lap, then he coasted to a stop at the finish line where the crowd had grown while he'd been driving. His chief helped him out of the harness, and he stood on his own feet, yanking off his helmet. He felt sore but happy. Accepting the back slaps and congratulations from his crew, his eyes were already glued on the tall brunette standing nearby.

He started toward her, the crowd parting as she ran to him and threw herself into his arms. Holding on tight, he spun them in a circle, loving how her sweet laughter filled the air.

"You better tell me right now, Bobby Winslow. I can't wait a minute more."

He pressed his lips to her ear. "I love you, Leeann Harris. I always have and I always will."

Her set her down but didn't let go. He couldn't, not when holding her felt so perfect. All he wanted was for the two of them to be alone, but the people who'd come to watch him had other ideas.

The questions came at him in a flurry. When Leeann started to inch away, he held tighter and looked down at her. "Don't go anywhere, okay?"

She nodded, her eyes bright. "They want you to say something about your test run, which to me looked pretty darn good."

Bobby smiled, enjoying the confidence and love in her voice, then turned to face the crowd. "If I could ask for a few minutes alone here with this pretty lady, I'll come back to you all with a special announcement that the citizens of Destiny will be the first to know."

He grabbed Leeann's hand and led her away from the cheering crowd, finding privacy on the other side of the trailer that housed his car. Before he said a word, he pulled his first and only love into his arms, lowered his mouth and gently kissed her.

A kiss Leeann returned, her hands strong and sure against his back as she leaned into his embrace. They clung to each other, forgiving past hurts and sharing unspoken promises.

Reluctant to release her, his lips wandered over her cheekbones, her eyelids and her forehead before he spoke. "I'm retiring from racing."

Leeann went still in his arms. "What? Did something happen out there?"

"The test run went perfectly."

"Then why? You don't have to do that."

Her words were warm on his neck. "I want to. It's time, it's the right decision."

"Is that what you plan to announce?" She leaned back to look at him. "Bobby, you need to be sure about this."

"I am sure, but there's a whole bunch of people I need to talk to before I can make it official, like my team, corporate sponsors and lawyers,"

Bobby said. "What I want to announce is the summer camp. Is that okay with you?"

Leeann nodded. "Everyone will be so excited."

"I want to tell them my wife and I will be—"

"Wife?"

He read surprise in Lee's beautiful eyes as she gazed up at him. This wasn't how he planned it. The ring he'd bought back in North Carolina was back at the house and he thought a walk to the pond...

"Bobby?"

"Marry me, Leeann." He reached for her hands and held tight. "So many things have changed for me this last year, but coming home, finding you, finding us again, is more than I'd ever hoped for. I've loved you my entire life and I can't imagine one more day without you."

"Yes."

"Yes?"

She laughed, the merry sound wrapping around them as she placed her hands to his cheeks and gave him another quick kiss. "Yes, I've loved you my entire life, too. Yes, I can't imagine one more day without you either, and yes, I'll marry you."

Her words settled deep in his heart, bringing with them a promise of an amazing future together. "I'm home, Leeann. Right here, right now with you. I'm finally home."

* * * * *